Hot Coded
by Nana

He reached for her and
dance, Jamie. Call a truce and it's one dance.
And you don't even have to leave your spot.
No one is watching you here in the corner."

She stared at his hand for a moment, then lifted her gaze
up to meet his. With a sigh, she slid her hand into his and
let him pull her into his body. "Fine. If it makes you go
away. Just one."

He nodded and pulled her closer against him, relishing
how they fit together. "How about for a little while we just
forget everything?"

Be Mine for Christmas
by Sheryl Lister

The moment the sexy stranger wrapped his arms
around her, sensations Maya never experienced
coursed through her body.

Her nerves were already on overload from his verbal play
at the table. She tried to pull away, but he tightened his
arms around her and held her closer to his hard body. She
resisted for a short moment, then brought her arms up
around his neck and melted into his embrace.

At length he said, "My apologies. I should have introduced
myself first. I'm Ian Jeffries…and you are?"

She lifted her head. "Maya. Maya Brooks."

Nana Malone is a *USA TODAY* bestselling author. Her love of all things romance and adventure started with a tattered romantic suspense she borrowed from her cousin on a sultry summer afternoon in Ghana at a precocious thirteen. She's been in love with kick-butt heroines ever since. And if she's not working or hiding in the closet reading, she's acting out scenes for her husband, daughter and puppy in sunny San Diego.

Books by Nana Malone

Harlequin Kimani Romance

Tonight with Sienna Mynx
A Vow of Seduction with Jamie Pope
Unwrapping the Holidays with Sheryl Lister

Visit the Author Profile page at
Harlequin.com for more titles.

Sheryl Lister has enjoyed reading and writing for as long as she can remember. She writes contemporary and inspirational romance and romantic suspense. She's been nominated for an Emma Award and the RT Reviewers' Choice Award, and named BRAB's 2015 Best New Author. Sheryl resides in California and is a wife, mother of three daughters and a son-in-love and grandmother to two very special little boys.

Books by Sheryl Lister

Harlequin Kimani Romance

It's Only You
Tender Kisses
Places in My Heart
Unwrapping the Holidays with Nana Malone

Visit the Author Profile page at
Harlequin.com for more titles.

NANA MALONE
SHERYL LISTER

UNWRAPPING
*T*HE
HOLIDAYS

WITHDRAWN
FROM
LONDON
PUBLIC LIBRARY

⊞HARLEQUIN®KIMANI™ ROMANCE

LONDON PUBLIC LIBRARY

If you purchased this book without a cover you should be aware that this book is stolen property. It was reported as "unsold and destroyed" to the publisher, and neither the author nor the publisher has received any payment for this "stripped book."

ISBN-13: 978-0-373-86473-7

Unwrapping the Holidays

Copyright © 2016 by Harlequin Books S.A.

The publisher acknowledges the copyright holders of the individual works as follows:

Hot Coded Christmas
Copyright © 2016 by Nana Malone

Be Mine for Christmas
Copyright © 2016 by Sheryl Lister

PLEASE RECYCLE
THIS PRODUCT IS RECYCLABLE

Recycling programs
for this product may
not exist in your area.

All rights reserved. The reproduction, transmission or utilization of this work in whole or in part in any form by any electronic, mechanical or other means, now known or hereinafter invented, including xerography, photocopying and recording, or in any information storage or retrieval system, is forbidden without written permission. For permission please contact Harlequin Kimani, 225 Duncan Mill Road, Toronto, Ontario M3B 3K9, Canada.

This is a work of fiction. Names, characters, places and incidents are either the product of the author's imagination or are used fictitiously, and any resemblance to actual persons, living or dead, business establishments, events or locales is entirely coincidental.

® and TM are trademarks of Harlequin Enterprises Limited or its corporate affiliates. Trademarks indicated with ® are registered in the United States Patent and Trademark Office, the Canadian Intellectual Property Office and in other countries.

For questions and comments about the quality of this book please contact us at CustomerService@Harlequin.com.

H HARLEQUIN®
™www.Harlequin.com

Printed in U.S.A.

CONTENTS

HOT CODED CHRISTMAS   7
Nana Malone

BE MINE FOR CHRISTMAS   113
Sheryl Lister

To Erik, thank you for that long-ago Christmas in London. I will forever remember my gift of apple jelly. You've always known how to make me happy.

Dear Reader,

Thank you so much for reading *Hot Coded Christmas*. After over a decade in the software world, I have a soft spot for my computer geeks. *Hot Coded Christmas* was a chance to revisit my old teams. Though I don't think any of my old engineers were nearly as hot as Cole!

Next up for me, I've got many more books. So sit back, relax and happy reading!

If you want to chat with me, I'm pretty easy to find!

Nana

www.nanamalone.com
www.Facebook.com/nanamalonewriter
www.Twitter.com/nanamalone

HOT CODED CHRISTMAS

Nana Malone

Chapter 1

Jamison Reed loved everything about Christmas.

From the decorations, to the songs, to the food, and yes, even fruitcake. She embraced it all. But now, as she watched her employees enjoy the Christmas party she'd catered, a long shadow cast a damper on her holiday.

How long would she be able to keep them all employed? Thanks to what she called the great screwup of her existence, she had fifty people she needed to take care of, and going into next year, she had no idea how to do it. *No*, that wasn't true. She had a Hail Mary plan, but what would she do if it didn't work? This was what she got for believing in love. A shattered heart and a drained corporate bank account.

Her head of marketing, Becca Long, sidled up to her, carrying two cups. "Eggnog for your troubles?"

Jamie gave Becca a small smile. "Thank you. Are you having fun?"

"Of course I am," she said, tossing her glossy dark hair over her shoulder. "I love the annual Christmas party. I love seeing who's drinking too much. I'm starting a pool on who's going to have the biggest hangover tomorrow. And I'm taking bets on who's going to lose their decorum first, once the music gets pumping." She shrugged. "There's at least one every year who forgets that this is a *work* party. But, yeah, I'm having fun. Way more than you. You look worried, boss lady."

Jamie sighed. That's because she *was* worried. Her small gaming company, Cyberpunked, had been having serious financial troubles. Their latest game had done extremely well, especially as it captured an audience of strong, sassy girls. But not exceptional enough to pull them out of the red. They had an investor in the wings willing to drop a ton of cash into the coffers, contingent on the potential of the next game. They'd evaluate everything based on their demo product.

They were willing to take a gamble if Cyberpunked's demo of the game garnered strong reviews and excitement. Only problem with that was, the demo was scheduled for mid-January and there was still a lot of testing to be done.

Jamison forced a smile for Becca. "I'm good, I promise. Just a little worried…" Becca was more than a friend though. She was a long-standing employee at the company. Over the years they'd grown close. But still, Jamie tried to shield her from the worst of it. From her epic blunders.

"If this is what good looks like, then I don't want any part of it. You look exhausted, girl. When was the last time you slept?" The petite brunette spread her arms open in front of the converted warehouse that served as Cyberpunked headquarters. The abundance of decorations made the space look like Santa had relocated the North Pole to their offices. "*This* is all great and everything, and I am so grateful that you did all this for us. I know you've been bending over backward to take care of the team, but you have to take care of yourself too. Don't think I missed how late you've been going home, or the midnight emails. Or how early you get up in the morning. I know you're killing yourself. And it pisses me off when I think about why."

Jamie shook her head. "No, Becca. Don't worry about me. Don't stress about anything. I promised to keep this place running and I will."

"Come on, Jamie, level with me. At least tell me how bad it is."

Jamie sighed. The truth would have everyone running for the unemployment line. "It's not good. But I don't want anyone to worry about it. When you guys all decided to stay, I can't even tell you what that meant to me. So, *I'm* going to handle it. You just focus on enjoying your Christmas holiday. We still have a couple of days to do everything we can for the game release, but then I want everyone to go and enjoy their two-week holiday. I'll take it from here."

Becca pursed her lips. "You do too much. But I know you're not going to listen to me." Her friend crossed her arms. "At least do me a favor and promise me you're going to do your best to enjoy the holiday?"

"I'll definitely try," she lied smoothly. She would enjoy her time off. It would just be a working holiday.

Becca didn't look like she believed her, but still her friend gave her a bright smile. "If you say so. Now, you drink your eggnog. I'm going to see if I can find a single hot guy in this crowd and some mistletoe."

Jamie had to laugh. With her good looks, Becca would have lots of takers.

"Enjoy." If the only thing Jamie had to worry about was finding someone to kiss for Christmas, her life would be so uncomplicated. *It was kissing that got her in this mess in the first place.* Matter of fact, mistletoe kissing had gotten her into a lot of trouble.

She took a sip of her eggnog, letting the cinnamon do its job to perk her up. Otherwise, she'd be groaning. She'd been an idiot, letting love enter into a business relationship. She and Brandon had started Cyperpunked over four years ago before they graduated college. By the time they were ready to don the cap and gown, they'd already put out a hugely successful game.

She'd thought they were on top of the world. How wrong she was. The two of them had met at Carnegie Mellon University their freshman year. She'd been one of the few women in her engineering class, and he'd been one of the rare attractive, sociable guys. And that year they'd had nearly every class together. They'd gravitated toward each other and bonded over their love of gaming. He'd always called her his sexy, cute gaming girl. Well, that had only lasted for so long.

After school, they'd moved to New York, where the start-up community was huge and funding was everywhere. They'd had a good run, but things had eventually fallen apart and it seemed Brandon had found another attractive, tech-savvy girl, because he'd left her for one of their interns. She'd come home from South by Southwest Festival to find him gone. He'd left a note. He'd wanted more excitement out of his life. What he'd really meant was he wanted an upgrade in girlfriends.

And to add salt to the wound, instead of just letting her buy him out, there'd been a fight over their clients.

Since he was in charge of sales and marketing, he'd managed to convince some of their biggest clients that he was the brains behind the shop.

His leaving hadn't been her fault. She was self-possessed enough to know that. But putting her company in a vulnerable position, *that* was her fault. She hadn't made him sign a freaking noncompete, the legal document that would have protected her stake. And she'd paid dearly for it. Not only had he taken their clients, but he'd also taken a good chunk of their employees with him. While she'd been building the business, he'd been polluting the well. When she'd fallen in love with him, she hadn't seen him for the master manipulator he was. And it had cost her too much.

Jamie had taken the high road, and refused to address the negative comments swirling on social media and around the building. Since she wouldn't respond, so many of them thought she wasn't in it to win it. They also worked with him directly, so why wouldn't they believe what he'd said? They'd eventually left with him.

With the team she had left, they'd managed to survive for the last year on the residuals from old games and revenue from some new games, but they were struggling and everybody knew it.

Especially Teched. The tech giant was breathing down her neck, eager for a takeover. They'd offered her a buyout, but she knew they would dismantle her company and fire half her employees. That was the general strategy of takeovers. She'd made her team a promise to keep the company going and she intended to keep it.

She wasn't ready to give up yet. Their last game had been hotly anticipated and the critics had loved it. It was doing well, and had stemmed the bleeding, but she needed a major infusion of cash pronto or there was no way she could keep the doors open.

She'd vowed that she would streamline her lifestyle before she would cut her team, but that promise was looking like a mistake. She'd eventually moved into the room at the back of the office to save on rent. How had she let this happen?

Stop it. You can do this. You can do anything. Besides, it's Christmas and you believe in miracles. So all you need is a miracle at Cyberpunked.

And her wish she would get. In two days, she would leave for her hometown in upstate New York. Since her family was away in France for her cousin's wedding, she'd hole up at Mountain Villas Lodge and work. She'd always wanted to stay there when she was a kid. She'd concentrate on the game and enjoy herself as much as she could. Her prayer would be answered, she knew it. It had to be. Because she wasn't going to give up on her company or herself.

Chapter 2

Cole Nichols pulled his Range Rover into the paved driveway of Mountain Villas Lodge.

The outer log facade gave the lodge a country effect, but he knew better. Inside, every room was state-of-the-art with the most modern of amenities. The main building housed two restaurants, a bar, a giant heart and seating areas.

They were nestled at the base of the mountain and when the snow fell thick, guests were immediately transported to a winter wonderland beautiful enough to rival any Disney could create.

A good portion of upstate New York had already seen its first snow. His family had bought into the lodge when he was a kid, so they always stayed in the owners' suite. He'd grown up just thirty miles from here, but this tiny town seemed like a lifetime away from the suburban hub he'd known. Or the urban setting he'd moved to. Out here, in Mills Spring, it was miles to the nearest neighbor. And deer, foxes and rabbits often made an appearance on the premises.

This year though, he'd be without his family or his would-be ex-fiancée. And right about now, he preferred it that way. Alone time with his laptop and the finest Scotch on earth was all he needed at this point.

The biting winter air snaked its way into his peacoat and he shivered. He'd left his damn scarf on the train from the city. But he'd survive. It wasn't like he was going to be leaving the property much.

He was taking a break from people. He needed solitude from everything. His Thanksgiving proposal hadn't quite gone according to plan so he was still smarting from that.

He wasn't a big lover of the holiday seasons and he wasn't going to miss not being with his family. His mother and stepfather had gone to Europe to ski this Christmas and he wasn't really in the mood for social-climbing ski bunnies at the moment.

He tried to shove the thought of his would-have-been fiancée out of his head. But he couldn't let go of the burn of rejection. She'd turned him down. *Him. Cole Nichols.* No one turned him down. But it wasn't so much that she'd turned him down, it was the reason she'd given him. That with all his money and connections, and his business, that she didn't think he could give her the lifestyle she wanted.

She wanted carte blanche to the accounts. And that wasn't going to fly on any day with him. She'd run through the monthly allowance he'd set up for her in a matter of days.

She liked to shop, and party and she wanted to look the part of a billionaire's girlfriend. He was generous, but it didn't matter how much he gave her, it was never enough.

Everyone had warned him about her. But like a fool, he thought he could change her. Control the situation.

She'd already replaced him with someone richer... older too. Someone who wouldn't bat an eyelash at her gold digger tendencies.

Fine by him. He wished her a lifetime of saggy butt wrinkles. Good riddance. He had work to do. And one day, she'd regret walking away from him. Truth was, he was more excited by the thought of his business goals right now anyway.

Teched was in the process of acquiring a small gaming firm that was bucking the system. Normally, he let his VP of acquisitions handle the takeovers and buyouts, but this damn CEO had been rejecting their offers for over a year. So Cole had gotten involved.

At first he thought it was funny that they declined. He knew the company was struggling, but somehow the owner had managed to keep Cyperpunked moving along. Cole would have preferred to avoid a messy situation, but all attempts to acquire them had been refused.

Fine by him—he liked a little fight anyway. Sooner or later they would buckle. He was going to spend the next two weeks gaining some leverage and applying some pressure.

He wasn't a fan of the word *no*. When it came to business, his father had taught him that someone who said no hadn't yet learned the benefits of saying yes. His father had also instructed him that when the cost outweighed the benefit, to walk away. Never get into a fight simply because someone irritated you. Maybe he hadn't learned that lesson so well.

In business, it was rare people said no to him. And

when they did, he usually was able to make them see things his way. There had been some deals he walked away from that became problematic, but not often. Cyberpunked was falling into that category. But for some reason he couldn't let it go.

He'd spent a year pursuing the company and so far, they'd rejected every offer he'd come up with. It equal parts infuriated as well as intrigued him. He'd found them out a few years ago with their game Spyder. The gaming kids had gone crazy over the realistic design and 3-D-level graphics. When he'd played it himself, he'd fallen in love with the labyrinth of scenarios and challenges in the game. The designers were smart. And they were playful and innovative too.

He'd made an attempt to secure the company then, but they'd refused to be bought. Six months later one of the partners took off with some of the major clients. The newly formed company built their own games and components for large game manufacturers as well. But the games they put out weren't as appealing as Cyberpunked's were. They were missing some of the nuance and complexity. Despite having the better product, Cyberpunked had limped along ever since.

The only logical conclusion was that the creative force behind that operation was the one left running the shop. And Cole wanted the shop. Well, mostly he wanted that key person on his team. The rest of the employees would probably be let go, or placed somewhere in his firm, but he didn't care about that. Cyberpunked thought they could fight the inevitable. But he knew better. He didn't give up on anything. And he wasn't going to start now. Come January, Cyberpunked was going to be part of Teched. They just didn't know it yet.

Chapter 3

As soon as Cole opened the door to his suite, his phone buzzed in his pocket. He grinned when he saw who it was. "Jake, what's up, man? Tell me you have good news."

"Define '*good* news'," Jake replied.

"Why is it every time you sound like that, I get the kind of information that puts me in a bad mood?"

His VP of acquisitions gave a humorless chuckle. "Because it's usually something comprised of the word *no*."

Cole ground his teeth. He at least wanted to do some skiing this afternoon before the work began. "What the hell is the matter now?"

"The latest offer to Cyberpunked was denied."

He pinched his nose. "Seriously? What the hell is their problem? The last package was beyond generous. Hell, it was practically a Christmas gift. I even made concessions for the engineering staff to be hired on."

Jake was silent for a moment. When he finally spoke, his words were slow, as if he'd measured each one before speaking. "Cole, maybe it's time to think about letting this one go. At least for the time being until they fall apart on their own. The terms are better for us if they come crawling for a bailout. I don't like this version of Teched, us chasing after a nothing game company. Hell, they have less than fifty employees. They aren't worth the effort. This is all ego to them."

Give up? The hell he would. "No, Jake. J.L. Reed is a genius. You played the game. You should understand."

"Look, I'm not saying the designer's not good. I'm just saying, we're getting nowhere. Right about now, the resources you're expending trying to get that company to pay attention to us are far outweighing the benefit. You don't usually get so stuck on something. This is going a step above and beyond. Maybe—"

Cole was quick to jump on the hesitation in his friend's voice. "Maybe what?"

"I'm just saying that maybe some of this has to do with Clarissa. You weren't able to hold on to her, good riddance by the way, but now you're desperate to attain this company. Maybe because the owner is female you think she should fall in line just like every other woman in your life."

Jake had been spending too much time with his psychologist girlfriend. That's what Cole thought. "You know, I appreciate the concern, but I know what I'm doing. We've been talking about a game division for years. This is the best foray into that."

Jake sighed. "I hear you, but what about the company that split from Cyberpunked? They are one-half of the outfit. And maybe they'll be less of a pain in the ass."

Cole was silent for a minute as he poured himself a

glass of Scotch. Most guys his age were indulging in craft cocktails. He had zero patience for adding basil and egg whites to a drink. And his tolerance was low for Jake right now. "Jake, have you ever known me to take less than the best?"

His friend sighed. "No."

"Then why would I take second best when the real brains are at Cyberpunked?"

"Okay. I hear you. I'll have another offer drawn up. Maybe it's time you asked for a personal appointment. Persuade the CEO to meet with you. Maybe she's old-school and needs a face-to-face. I know she declined to meet with the proposal team. But a meeting request from you directly could tip the scales."

For the first time in the conversation, Jake was saying something that made sense. Cole could really state his case then. And in person, there were few people who would tell him no. "Best thing you've said to me all day."

"Okay, I'll get on it. And Cole?"

"Yeah?"

"For once, try and enjoy the holiday."

Like hell that was happening. "Not likely, but you get me that company for Christmas and it'll go a long way toward improving my mood." Everywhere he went, people tried to insist he should be festive. Relax. But they didn't understand how much he hated the season. It had been years since he could enjoy it.

"Working on it."

As soon as Cole hung up, he didn't even get to pick up his glass before the room phone rang. "Yes?"

It was the front desk. "So sorry to disturb you, Mr. Nichols, but there is a problem that needs your attention."

"Really? Can't the on-site manager handle this?" He'd hired a management company so he could stay in the background of everything. If his mother had her way, she'd have nothing to do with the place. Too many memories of his father.

"Not this time, sir."

"Fine, I'll be right there." So far his relaxing vacation was anything but.

This was not happening. "What do you mean you are overbooked? That is not possib—" Jamie had to stop herself from cussing out the guy behind the reservation desk. He looked young. Like just-out-of-high-school young. Screaming at him would get her nowhere. And she was so worked up she might trigger an asthma attack.

She tried some yoga techniques to regulate her breathing. Nope, that didn't work. She was still furious. "So what do you suggest I do? You're looking at my reservation aren't you? I mean it's there, but somehow you're telling me that you have nowhere to put me?"

His hands shook as he stammered. "I—I—I'm so sorry, miss, but there are no empty rooms. One of the guests extended a week and that was meant to be your suite. I'm terribly sorry. We'd like to comp you a free stay—"

She could feel the pressure building and could almost sympathize for the kid...*almost.* Except now he was offering her something that would be useless. Forget Zen. She needed to work. Right now. "Okay. Sure, what's going to happen is you're going to comp my next stay, though why I would ever stay here after this is beyond me."

"I wish I had a solution for you. If I had a room available I'd rent it to you."

Still mad, she was feeling punchy and so exhausted from the trip. "Well, then, you're going to go and get in your car and take me to your place and you will find some other accommodation for the week."

His eyes went wide. He thought she was kidding. Or crazy. Truth was she was that desperate. "M-m-my place?"

Jamie nodded. "Yep. When do we leave?"

"But—but where would *I* stay?"

Jamie smirked. "Well, since you don't seem to care about where *I'll* stay, I am finding it hard to give two figs about where *you'll* stay." She shouldered her bag. "Okay, I'm ready to go when you are."

Poor kid looked ready to pee himself. *Be nice, Jamison. It's not his fault.* She sighed. "Okay, look, I'll let you have the couch."

Somehow that didn't mollify him. Go figure.

"You can't stay with me."

"What happened to the holiday spirit? You're going to turn a defenseless woman out onto the streets with nowhere to go?" She was far from helpless but he didn't know that. Her mother had sold their house three years ago to move to California. Otherwise she'd just go home. She could hack her way into some hotel's reservation system, but since it was the holiday season, hotel rooms were scarce. She wouldn't do that to someone.

"No, I—"

A deep baritone came from behind her. Smooth as silk, and low and mellow enough to warm her from the outside chill. "What seems to be the problem?"

The kid's whole body sagged in relief as if thrilled to be able to hand her off to someone else to handle.

Jamie, on the other hand, tensed. She knew that voice. Knew it well. It had been years, but she'd never forget it. She whirled around. *Cole. Freaking. Nichols.* The object of every schoolgirl fantasy. Come to life... in the flesh. But unlike her fantasies...he was clothed. Bummer.

Also, unlike her fantasies, he was likely to speak... which would ruin everything.

He blinked at her and his brows quickly furrowed.

Jamie tipped her chin up. Was he really going to act like he had no idea who she was? Not that she should be surprised, but still.

He stared at her for a moment too long, but Jamie was determined not to give in. She wasn't looking away. If he was going to stare, then she could stare too.

First thing she noticed was that he looked good. But then Cole Nichols had always looked good. He'd been a football god, the kind of guy that even smart, ambitious girls noticed. Problem was he was also brilliant. His skills were phenomenal enough to have been in competition with her for every single academic award or acknowledgment in high school.

He had played football with her brother, Matt, and like the other guys on the team had spent a good deal of time at her house because her mother was team Mom, but it wasn't like he and she were besties. He was always there, either he nipping at her heels or she chasing him. Until their paths connected and crossed at that end-of-semester party.

You will not think about that party. No. That was ancient history. What she did allow herself to remember about Cole was he was good-looking, rich and, oh yeah, an asshole.

But that was a long time ago. He might have changed.

Jamie took a step forward, but instead of marble-tiled floor, her foot caught nothing but air. In the seconds between being on her feet and falling backward, so many thoughts ran through her head. Thoughts like: *This would only happen to you.* And: *Maybe you'll get lucky and the floor will swallow you.* And finally: *Of course the next time you see him and you're flat on your behind.*

Though a final look at his face before her rear made contact with the marble told her all she needed to know. From the look on his face, nothing had changed.

She used several inventive curses to illustrate just how she felt, and he whistled low. "Looks like Jamison Reed finally grew up. Who taught you to swear, Jamison?"

Okay, in her case, she was going to look him in the pecs, then work her way up to his eyes. *Yeah, hell of a plan.* "It's Jamie. And in case you were wondering, I'm fine."

His lips quirked into a wry smile. "I see some things never change."

No. Apparently they didn't. Because he looked just as mouthwatering as he had the last time she'd seen him, seven years ago.

He'd cut his hair though, a style that was shorter on the sides and a bit longer on top, sort of a messy mohawk. It was stylish, just like his peacoat and Cole Haan boots. She recognized the boots because her brother had the same pair. Just her luck. Cole Nichols was still more gorgeous than the devil himself...and he was speaking to her...after seven years.

Jamie blinked hard to clear her head and not think of the last time she'd spoken to him.

"Sorry. Are you okay?" His voice was soft, gentle... almost.

Besides her bruised behind? She was not going to

tell him about the state of her butt. "I'm fine. Or I will be when your employee over here realizes that until he finds me a room, I'll be bunking with him."

Cole chuckled low as he helped her up. "That won't be necessary. Since you're in the predicament because the property screwed up, you can stay in the owners' suite…with me."

Her eyes went wide. She might not have heard that correctly. Stay with him? Like, as in, with him, *Cole Nichols*? She shook her head "I—I—I can't do that." Especially not given she remembered every single detail of the last time they'd spoken.

He narrowed his eyes and Jamie got the impression that no one ever told him no. But when he spoke, his voice was calm, restrained. "Well, for starters, you won't find another hotel with vacancies this close to Christmas. And second, the main suite is nearly a thousand square feet. I don't need that much space."

"B-but we…you…I—" She was a smart woman who knew words. *Lots* of words. Just not ones she could think of right now. "I have work to do and intrusions will be distracting and…" Her voice trailed.

His lips twisted into a wry smile. "I see the cat's got your tongue. But call it the holiday spirit or whatever." He shrugged then bent down to help her retrieve the contents that had spilled from her purse. As he shoved her phone and her inhaler back into her purse and handed it back to her, he asked, "Have you got any other options?"

Her inner adult scowled at the inner giddy teenager who was excited about this development. She was annoyed. But she could do this. Especially as she had no other choice. Jamie sighed. "Fine. Merry Christmas, roomie."

Chapter 4

You are an idiot.

The last thing on earth Cole wanted was company this holiday. Jamison Reed kind of company. Especially not since she practically screamed Christmas, with the red-and-green-colored stripes in her hair and her reindeer sweater. Oh yeah, and she signified everything he wanted to forget about that time in his life.

But where the hell else is she supposed to go? Yes, that. And this was Jamison. Matt Reed's little sister. Back in high school, Matt had been his tight end on the football team. And his sister had always been around at team functions. And she'd outsmarted him for half the scholarships the school had to offer. Every time an academic competition was announced, the two of them were right there, neck and neck. Until his life turned upside down.

They hadn't exactly run in the same circles, but she'd always been there. As Cole walked her back to the suite, the bellboy trailing in their wake, he tried not to remember all the little details he knew about her.

Things he didn't need to remember. Like she was only eleven months behind her brother so they'd been in the same year in school. Details like how cute she was. Spunk and brains in a tiny package. Barely five feet three inches, she'd been a little dynamo.

But the number one thing he really didn't want to remember? That smart mouth of hers. Yeah, probably best he didn't think about her mouth.

She was one of those happy, bubbly kinds of people. Always looking at the positive slant on things. Always optimistic. He'd never understood her. Mostly, he'd kept a wide berth. Until that party.

Sure, he and her brother had been teammates, but they hadn't been super tight. Even then, he'd understood the rules of the team. No one messed with anyone's family. *Too bad you broke that rule.*

And now like a moron, he'd invited her to stay with him. As in, within feet of *him*. The scent of her apple-and-ginger shampoo would drive him nuts. Not that he had been trying to pay attention to what she smelled like. Whenever she was standing right next to him, it was impossible not to notice.

She was exactly like he remembered, different streaks in her hair maybe, but her skin was the same brushed cinnamon and her dark eyes still all knowing.

She'd looked at him with such focus that he was convinced she could see every thought. But the thing that still got him were her lips. They were full and soft. And he wondered if she still used strawberry lip gloss.

What? No. He was not going there again. The last thing he needed was that kind of distraction. Hell, she'd probably forgotten all about that night anyway. But the masochistic part of him hoped she hadn't.

He opened the door for her and she whispered a "Thank you." The bellboy went in next and Cole directed him to the loft bedroom just up the stairs. After he'd tipped the young man and Jamie set her laptop case on the counter, he shrugged, ready to show her where things were. But she spoke first.

"Th-thank you for this. I wasn't entirely sure what I was going to do. Probably camp out in the lodge or something. You saved my behind."

"Like I said, I have the room. And it's no problem. *We* messed up the reservation so it was my responsibility to fix it. Besides, you're a friend, of sorts."

Her eyes went wide and his skin pricked with heat. Was she going to call him on what happened with them all those years ago?

But she didn't. Instead, she said, "I—uh notice you haven't decorated yet. You want some help putting all the stuff up?"

Her smile was overly bright and it was apparent that, unlike him, she was looking forward to Christmas. "Uh, well, I just got in myself. Besides, I'm not really a holiday person."

"What?" Her mouth hung open.

A chuckle burst forth before he could stop it. She just looked so gobsmacked. "Sorry. You act like I just personally killed Santa. Not really my thing."

"No tree, no lights, no gingerbread houses? No mistletoe or eggnog?"

"Sorry. No."

"I just—" She shook her head. "Okay, fine. You just show me where all the stuff is and I'll get it all set up for you. It's the least I can do. Bring in a little Christmas cheer."

Silent alarm bells clanged in his head. Oh no. Not going to happen. "No, it's really not necessary. I'm really here to work anyway so—"

She waved a hand at him dismissively. "So am I, but working doesn't mean we can't do Christmas. I *love* the holidays. Show me where it all is. I'll do the setting up. If you can make sure I'm not sleeping in my car for the holiday, I can do a little decorating. And we need to get you an ugly sweater. Maybe there's one in the gift shop."

Cole stared at her, caught somewhere between laughter and bewilderment. She hadn't changed a bit. She still talked a mile a minute with a determination that was unstoppable. Problem was, he wasn't sure if that was a good thing or not. Either way though, he knew it would be easier to let her have her way. He could deal. And it wasn't like he needed to wrap presents or anything. "Fine, all the stuff is in the storage closet down the hall, next to the garage. If you want a tree, I can have one brought in."

"A real tree? I brought my tiny miniature one, but that would be even better."

He blinked. "You travel with your own Christmas tree?" He put his hands up. "You know what? Never mind. Okay, I'll call and have it brought in."

She grinned and in that minute, she looked every bit the fun eighteen-year-old she'd been. "Cool, you just let me take care of everything."

He stared after her as she pranced down the hall. This was a mistake. He could feel it in his bones. But there wasn't much he could do to stop the train.

Jamie rested her hand on the wall of the storage room, the dust particles dancing in the streams of light.

Holy hell, she'd just agreed to stay *here* with Cole. *You. Are. An. Idiot.*

You were thinking you have work to do and don't have time to run around trying to find a place to sleep. But Cole? This was stupid. How was she supposed to ignore that undercurrent for a *week*? Let alone ten days. Was it possible to die from embarrassment? Or longing? That had to be a real thing right?

Focus, Jamison. Get the decorations up and then you can work. And maybe even enjoy a little bit of Christmas. She'd been expecting to be in a basic room. She couldn't believe Cole had a luxury suite and wasn't using it to go all out on the holiday celebration.

The ceiling soared and the color palette was a very contemporary shade of yellow. The furniture was contemporary and light. But there was so much texture. Cotton, flannel throws, a pop of velvet here. And then of course, there was the enormous fireplace serving as the focal point. And the massive iron-and-glass lighting fixture up above made the room dance in light.

And the far wall was made entirely of glass. If she looked hard enough, she'd likely see deer roaming the property.

She'd get some stuff set up, then do some work. Maybe bake some cookies as a reward. The kitchen was all kitted out with granite counters and the nicest appliances she'd ever seen. Not that Cole looked like he planned on taking advantage of them.

Do what you came to do, not to reminisce about Cole. What happened was stupid kid stuff. It belongs in the past.

But as Jamie pushed away from the wall and started to unpack the boxes of lights, her mind automatically took her back to that long-ago night.

Frank O'Connor's parties were sort of legendary. That night, things hadn't gotten into full swing yet because the basketball team had been at an away game and was delayed. So her brother wasn't there yet. It was mostly a bunch of bored kids sitting around drinking.

Nothing extraordinary until Marcie Gates, Frank's girlfriend, suggested they make things exciting with some spin the bottle. Or at least a version of it.

A lot of interesting things had happened after that. Frank and Marcie got in a huge argument because he'd had too much fun making out with Carrie Moss in the closet and she'd let Fitz Jacobson touch her boobs.

Jamie hadn't even wanted to play really. She'd just been down there holding her first beer, trying to blend in with the cool kids before Matt arrived. If he'd seen her he'd have flipped out and told their parents. And there would have been a ban on all future parties. As big brothers went, he was pretty overprotective.

Usually, she didn't even go to parties unless Matt was there. Not like anyone thought to invite her. Sure, she was Matt's sister, so she was accepted into the cool-kids crew by his insistence, but she wasn't one of them. Not one of the pretty people. But when Marcie had asked her if she was going, she'd said yes and dragged her friend Claire with her. Too bad Claire had ditched her in favor of giggling with one of the hockey players.

Cole had been there. Hell, he was *always* there in the background. As was the way with banes of existence. If he told her brother that she'd been drinking, she'd be toast. Just her luck, when it was her turn, the spinning bottle had landed on the empty space that he walked right into. Even now she could feel the heat on her face as he'd studied her.

A moment later, he'd been dragging her into the

closet to read her the riot act about being irresponsible, and drinking and how she should know better. It was like dealing with Matt. Of course he'd pointed out that she'd been drinking at a party with no one looking out for her. He'd gone on and on about how things would be perceived by other people. She could still remember struggling against his hold and muttering, "I'm not drinking. I've been muscling through the first sips of this beer to fit in with everyone. I don't know how you guys can drink that stuff."

He really hadn't liked it when she pointed out that by dragging her into the closet, things didn't look good for either of them.

It was clear to everyone on the outside that they weren't making out so Frank insisted they could come out only if they actually made out.

Jamie's skin still burned at the memory. It was like they all knew she was the squeaky-clean good girl. As if she wore it like a brand.

Cole had just rolled his eyes and told her to sit down and be quiet for a few minutes and Frank would eventually let them out.

"Are you serious right now?"

He'd scoffed. "Frank's being a prick, but you're Matt's sister so he won't mess with you too much. Just moan at the door or something."

Jamie frowned. "What?"

"You know, moan, like you're doing something fun."

She'd tried, but she sounded more like she was in pain than any of the sexy moans she'd heard in movies.

"Geez, Jamison, it's like you have no idea how to pretend like you're having a good time."

Frank had banged on the door again to remind them of what they were supposed to be doing.

She threw up her hands. "I have no idea how to do it. I've never hooked up with anyone before," she spilled. "So why don't you try your hand at moaning?"

He blinked. "Bull."

She shook her head. "No bull. So, I'm sorry I don't have it right or whatever." Jamie recalled Cole's eyes raking over her inducing a wave of heat as if it were yesterday.

Cole had banged his head against the back of the closet and squeezed his eyes shut. "You have to at least have kissed someone right? I heard you were going out with Adam Sinclair or something."

She ducked her head. "I—uh. I'm not too sure Adam likes girls. At least he doesn't like me. He didn't want to kiss me." She shrugged. "I figured I just didn't do it for him or something."

"What?" He'd brought his head up. "You think it's you? No. It's not you. It's him."

"Yeah, well it feels like it's me. Heck, no one's asking for my number or seems particularly interested, so…" Jamie let her voice trail.

Cole had run his hands through his hair. "I get it. You want to be noticed. But people notice you. Right now, I bet there's some poor guy wishing you'd look at him. I'd rather you talk with him than one of these drunken varsity kids. Sometimes guys can take advantage." Then he peered at her through thick lashes. "What are you waiting for anyway? A kiss is no big deal."

She'd ignored his last question. "You're one of those varsity kids. Are you taking advantage of me?" she asked.

"Unlike you, I haven't been drinking. And you're Reed's little sister. It's different."

"Great. Just what I need. Another big brother. I keep going like this and I'll never get my first kiss."

Cole groaned. "Just stop. It'll happen. You know, when you're at college. Far away from anywhere Matt can kick someone's ass."

She'd licked her lips nervously and gathered every ounce of bravery she possessed. "Or maybe you could do it."

His eyes had locked with hers, but he'd shaken his head. "No can do, Jamison."

"It's Jamie. And why not? You obviously know what you're doing if Rebecca Watts can be believed. And you said it yourself, it's not like it means anything. I'm not going to be some dopey girl that chases after you. And bonus, not like I'll be chasing you around begging you to do it again."

She had been lying through her teeth of course. Because sometimes when she was all alone, she wondered what it would be like to kiss him. It was silly. He never even noticed her other than as competition. She could count on one hand the number of one-on-one interactions they'd had. But she'd always been hyperaware of him.

"If you do it, I'll stay away from jocks at parties and I'll stop pretending to drink." Beer tasted like piss to her. "I just want to know."

Cole swallowed hard, his brows furrowed. "If I do this, you never tell Matt? And you stop trying to make out with varsity assholes."

"Yeah, okay."

"And promise me. No more even holding a can of beer. And beware of frat boys bearing fruit punch. You understand me? You're way too trusting."

"Deal."

Cole shook his head and patted the carpet next to him. "It'll be easier if you sit. Because you're practically puppet-sized."

She wrinkled her nose. "I am not."

"Uh-huh." When she sat, he wrapped an arm around her shoulders and she relished his warmth. "You want the guy to treat you like you're special. Be gentle with you. Never coming on too strong, okay?"

She nodded. Taking mental notes. "Got it."

Then Cole had caressed a cheek with his thumb and cupped the back of her neck under her hair and angled her head. Her heart was thundering so loud, she could barely hear him when he spoke.

"Okay. I'm pretending it's not you, Jamison."

Her first kiss had turned molten hot in seconds as he schooled her in how to kiss. How she should expect to be touched. Everything had been so gentle, passionate, and she wanted more.

Blood rushing in her head and heart hammering, she'd decided to take matters into her own hands. She pulled back, and he frowned but let her go easily. "Are you okay?"

At first all she could manage was a nod. But then she blurted. "Yeah, but I want you to really kiss me. I know you're holding back."

Cole tucked a piece of hair behind her ear. "Jamison. You don't want—"

"Yes, I do. Or some other guy is going to teach me and he won't have my best interest at heart…" When it looked like he might not kiss her properly, she pushed herself into a crouch and levered herself onto his lap facing him. "Please show me."

"I—" Then he sighed and kissed her again. The second time around hadn't been quite so gentle. His lips had been far more urgent, his hand skimming up her tank top to run his thumbs just over her ribs. The tease of his thumb over each ridge sent a shiver through her body.

His hand clamped on her hips and he set the tempo of the kiss and their rocking bodies.

The sensations zipping through her body weren't just new. Try explosive and mind changing. She knew she couldn't go back. Not to boring, bland her. Not when she knew it was possible to feel this way.

The tingles wrapped around her spinal chord tight and forced her muscles to bunch. Forced her body to arch, searching for…something.

Cole kissed her deep. His hand on her hip moving her until their bodies rocked into each other again and again. But then he threw his head back against the wall and tucked her against him.

She'd tried to ask him why he stopped. Or what she'd done wrong. The evidence of his arousal was hard to miss. And the idea that she'd managed to excite him was heady. But when she tried to talk, he hushed her, then held her for what felt like an eternity.

They didn't move until the sounds of the party were in full swing. Then he'd gently lifted her away. His motions stiff and jerky. "You okay?"

She lied as smoothly as she could. "Yeah, I'm fine. You?"

"To tell you the truth, I have no idea."

"I'm sorry. I didn't—"

He'd kissed her forehead then. "You have zero reason to be sorry. None. Let's go."

He'd taken her out of the closet and it seemed like everyone had forgotten the game. She left that room with him feeling anxious and curious. But the longing was most prevalent.

That party had marked the beginning of winter break. And considering her parents had dragged them to Saint Louis that Christmas, she hadn't seen him again until the following January.

And then it was like it never happened. She wasn't sure exactly how these things should go, but he was silent. The weird part was, he ignored *everyone*. Quit track, didn't run soccer and left all his academic clubs. She'd easily made valedictorian after that. Not exactly how she'd wanted to do it. It was obvious something was wrong. But the one time she'd tried to approach him, he'd looked through her. Like she didn't exist. She hadn't tried again. And now, he was playing savior to her damsel in distress? How the heck was she supposed to survive a day with him, let alone ten days?

Chapter 5

Jamie was a Christmas-decorating expert. A pro short on time, so, she did the basics. Stuck some battery-operated candles in the windows, put up the wreaths. Strung some garlands and pinned a few snowflakes to the ceiling. She pulled out the nativity scene to place under the tree.

It only took her about an hour after the tree had arrived. The whole time Cole had been absent. She hadn't seen a glimpse of him since he'd brought her in. After she was done, she settled in to get some work done. Working, for her, was like going into another zone. She didn't even like people around because it messed with her flow too much. She usually employed noise-canceling headphones and played nature sounds. She changed to music once she got her groove. Today, for sure, called for Christmas music.

After picking her spot on the couch, and setting up

the router configuration, she was pretty much up and running. She was so deep into issues to mark for fixing that she didn't notice when Cole had come out from one of the rooms down the other hallway.

It wasn't until his shadow loomed over her that she snapped her head up.

When she jumped he grinned. Tugging the noise cancelers off, she smiled sheepishly. "Sorry about that. When I'm working I go total focus mode."

"Yeah, I caught that. I've been trying to get your attention for five minutes. Of course that was before I realized you'd gone into la-la land or whatever." He glanced around. "I see you were dead serious about decorating. Looks like a Christmas vortex in here."

"Bah humbug, Scrooge." She rolled her eyes. "I can't believe you don't get into Christmas." Shoot, unless he was Jewish. "Damn, I didn't even ask if your family even celebrated Christmas. Maybe you do Hanukkah or Kwanzaa or something and here I am with my nativity scenes."

He coughed a laugh. "No, we did Christmas. It was a pretty big deal in my house, the hot cocoa, ice-skating on Christmas Eve. The whole thing."

She frowned as she looked up at him. "So what happened? Did an elf scare you when you went to sit on Santa's lap one year?"

A shadow crossed over his face and for a moment, he looked so vulnerable and lost. But then it was gone and he cleared his throat. "Nah, I'm just grown now. I know there's no such thing as Santa Claus."

She hadn't imagined it. There *was* a shadow of pain behind his eyes, but he didn't seem interested in talking about it. Of course, to someone like her, that just made her want to ferret it out and fix the bug. The *defective* code. Right the imperfection. *Not your business.*

So instead, she just said, "What? I refuse to believe there's no Santa. I insist on believing in the jolly man with the beard and Rudolph. Except in my mind, Santa looks like a male model, and has a six-pack."

The hint of a smile was back on his lips. "You want to interview for Mrs. Claus, then?"

She laughed. "I don't do relationships." *At least not anymore.* "Just like you don't do Christmas."

"Fair enough." He inclined his head toward the front door. "I guess with your earphones on, you didn't hear the front door. I had pizza delivered. I'm at a good stopping point if you are and want to eat."

She lifted her brows. "Sure. I could eat, but then, I can always eat."

His brows went up. "You're so tiny though."

"I am small but mighty."

He smirked. "Anyway, if you want some help with some of the lights, we can do that before we eat."

Jamison couldn't believe her ears. "Mr. Bah Humbug wants to help?"

He shrugged. "You're the size of an elf—you'll never be able to get them up there. Besides, your sweater might catch fire with all those lights. And you seem super into it, so whatever."

She glanced down. "This sweater is awesome. You're just jealous they don't have one this cool down in the gift shop for you. But you know what, I'll find one for you, as a thank-you."

His brow furrowed. "I'm good. You don't need to thank me any more."

Jamie glanced at her laptop and hit Save out of habit. The system autosaved her project, but she wasn't taking any chances. "Oh, but I *really*, *really* want to." Laughing as she stood, she had to crane her neck to look up at him.

Stretching out her muscles, she worked out the kinks as she followed him toward the aroma of pepperoni pizza. Her stomach rumbled.

"Okay, maybe we'll get food first, then."

Jamison laughed. "You don't mind, do you?"

"Nope. Given the roar of your belly, I don't want to see what happens if I don't feed you." He pulled down the plates and glasses and grabbed a couple of sodas out of the fridge.

This was weird and at the same time totally normal. Like they did this all the time. Nevermind the pink elephant in the room. Jamison thought she'd be more nervous talking to him, but he was so much mellower than she remembered. There was still an intensity to him and her skin still prickled with heat every time she felt his gaze on her, but this she could do. Act like a normal person and not a hormonal teenager.

Normal… Right. Besides, she had a hell of a lot of work to do. She'd run into a glitch in the maze. She was missing something, but she couldn't quite put her finger on it. It was technically fine, but she didn't do fine. Fine was not in her vocabulary. It needed to be outstanding. She needed a miracle so she had to be better than fine.

"You're frowning. Why?"

Cole's voice had a way of melting through her inner dialogue with herself. "Shoot, sorry, when I'm working, I tend to get all in my head and forget I'm meant to be talking to real people. Bad habit. So why don't you tell me all about Cole Nichols. And not the boring sanitized school, work, location stuff. Real stuff. Like where are all the bodies buried."

He laughed. "What makes you think I'd tell you that? For all you know you'll be joining them."

"I'm pretty sure I could take you. I'm small but mighty." She took another delicate bite.

Cole's eyes narrowed and sharpened on her lips. When he spoke, his voice was harsher, deeper. "You're the size of a Smurf." He looked like he wanted to say something else but snapped his mouth shut. His gaze locked with hers. The intensity of it nearly scorching her skin.

She *should* look away from him…except she couldn't. If she wasn't careful, she'd soon be doing that uncomfortable staring thing and he would know she was crazy. "I'll take that to mean I'm sprightly! And sprightly wins over dark and broody any day."

"I am not dark and broody." He scoffed.

"I know your shtick. You act all bah humbugy, but you're a good guy. After all, you let a relative, Christmas-loving, stranger stay with you when you were clearly not in the Christmas mood. Someone like that wouldn't have bodies buried out back."

Cole just shrugged. "You're supposed to help elves. It's like a Christmas rule or something."

"Don't think I don't recognize deflection when I see it."

It was a good thing Cole Nichols didn't walk around with a grin all the time; women everywhere would be left quivering in his wake. The flash of teeth and the crinkling of his eyes at the corners and she was about to melt in a pool of warm gooeyness. "I have to remember you're sharper than most."

"Come on, no little details about what you've been up to all this time?"

He shook his head. "Not much to say if I can't talk about work or where I live or where I went to school."

Jamie stared at him. "Oh come on, no adventures, hiking the Andes, BASE jumping off the Eiffel Tower, no supermodel girlfriend in Antibes or Saint-Tropez? You're ruining my image of the mysterious Cole Nichols."

His laugh was quick. "I'm not mysterious. I'm an open book."

Jamie raised a brow. "Okay, so what's your deal—girlfriend, married? Why are you spending the holiday alone?" *Why did you ask that? Why?* A muzzle would be a good idea.

The teasing glint went out of his eyes in an instant. His one-word answer said it all. "Nope." And the subject change was so quick it gave her whiplash. "You ready to put up those lights now? Or do you want the last piece?"

She glanced down at the pizza. Between the two of them they'd managed to eat seven of eight slices. Three of them she'd eaten herself. "Yeah, the lights seem like a good idea."

Lights. Yes, more decorating. Then she'd get back to work. Deal with the task in front of her. Do what she came to do. Not drool over Cole. Because, well, she really should have learned her lesson by now.

For the next ten minutes, they worked in relative companionship. He even smiled once or twice. He might not like Christmas but he was letting her enjoy hers, which was pretty decent of him.

She turned to ask him for the next set of lights, but her foot slipped on the stool.

In a flash, Cole wrapped both arms around her, bringing his body flush against hers, and Jamison

lost everything she'd perhaps ever had in her brain.
Gone. Poof.

Jamie sucked in a deep breath. Cole stood statue-like
as his hands flexed across her back. Tension wrapped
around them, then crackled and Jamison didn't know
when she'd so acutely felt every feminine instinct.

He quickly held her away an inch, but if she dared
breathe again, her nipples were going to rub against his
chest. She could feel his hands moving behind her as
they stood, gazes locked, bodies not otherwise moving.
Holy hell. Cole Nichols was just about the sexiest man
she'd ever seen in her life. Easy does it. *Remember last
time you went down this path?*

Sure, he had an angled, sculpted jaw and cheekbones
that made supermodels jealous and his dark lashes
framed clear dark eyes. And of course there was the
hair. It just looked soft to the touch. And there was no
forgetting his body. She wondered if his abs still had
abs. More than once when she'd been a teenager, she'd
lost time just by trying to count them. She always got a
little distracted around four and had to start recounting.

But for her, the pinnacle of sexiness lay in Cole's
lips. His lips endlessly fascinated her. Back then. Not
now. Because now she was an adult who knew better.
They were full and curved in a hint of a mysterious,
devilish smile. It was that smile that had her drooling
all over him years ago. It was those lips that made her
want to misbehave.

And right now they were inches from hers. If she
tipped up her face *and* stood on tiptoe *and* climbed up
his body, she could press her lips to his. But Cole Nichols was not on the menu. *You're here to work.*

So distracted by his lips, she forgot about keeping
her boobs to herself; she released the breath she'd been

holding. When her breasts brushed against his chest she clamped her jaw tight to stop herself from moaning. But one escaped anyway.

Cole's eyes had fluttered shut but other than that, he was doing an excellent statue impression.

When he opened them again, she saw annoyance, confusion and something else. It looked like hunger. But that couldn't be right. She cleared her throat, and then stepped down off the stool, out of his arms. "I guess I'm done with these lights." She nervously licked her lips.

His voice was rough when he spoke. "You okay?"

She nodded slowly. "Yeah. Good. Great even." Cue awkward silence.

"Sorry about the tree. A few branches broke when it fell."

"No big deal, I can get the fake one out of the closet."

"I can cut one from the property if you want. It's one of the services we offer guests."

"God, no, you don't have to do all that. I just wanted to get into the spirit since I'm working and all. I don't need you to cut me down a tree."

He shoved his hands in his back pockets. "You never said why you were all alone for the holiday."

There was no way she was getting into that right now. "Long story. Family is in France and I am hoping for a Christmas miracle."

"Now who's being mysterious?"

What the hell was wrong with him? Cutting down a tree? It had been *years* since he'd done this. His hands hurt. And his back was *killing* him. Hell, had it been this hard when he was a kid? Probably because his father had done the lion's share of the work and he'd made snow angels.

But it was all worth it when he used the sled to drag the tree into the house. Jamie squealed and clapped. "Oh my God, it's perfect." If only it was this easy to make all women happy.

He'd never seen anyone so delighted over a damn tree. He was supposed to be working. A drink in his hand, basketball on in the background, laptop in his lap. That was the plan. Getting a Christmas tree wasn't part of the equation.

But look how happy it made her.

The scent of cinnamon wafted in the air. "What's that smell?"

She glanced toward the kitchen. "Oh, well, you took a little longer than I thought, so I started on a batch of my mom's cinnamon cookies."

"I really am rooming with a Christmas elf."

"You bet." She grinned at him, all white teeth and dimples.

She hummed Christmas songs as she pulled out a tray of cookies. And despite himself, Cole was starting to remember when Christmas had been fun. "So given your unholy love of the holiday, how did you end up all alone on Christmas? And don't give me any bull about working."

She rolled her eyes even as she laughed. "It is not an unholy love." She tossed a piece of popcorn at him, which he dodged. "Fine. Bad breakup. That unsettled me a little. Then I've been so consumed with work that I haven't really come up for air, so no time to plan something major. The family was headed for a big trip, but I just couldn't do that and stay focused."

He knew the feeling. "As of Thanksgiving I was single, so not really in the people kind of mood."

She frowned. "I'm sorry. What happened? Hotter supermodel came along?"

Despite himself, his lips twitched. "*No.* That was the month before," he teased. "She broke up with me."

"Oh damn. I'm sorry." She winced. "Sometimes my mouth runs away from me."

"No, you're good. I probably should have seen it coming. She showed more day-to-day interest in my stock portfolio than I did." She was easy to talk to. Too easy.

"Ah, so she had her sights set on a billionaire."

He laughed. "Yeah, I guess."

"Well, her loss. I think millionaires have a lot to offer. If only women would give them a chance."

He laughed and he threw a piece of popcorn at her. "You're funny."

"I mean, I'm just saying, when did millionaires go out of style?"

"Right?" he laughed. "I mean, I should be able to have at least two supermodel girlfriends."

He didn't manage to dodge the popcorn she threw at him. One kernel hit him right on the nose. "You are gonna get it."

She squared her shoulders, and then put down the sewing needle she'd been using to thread the popcorn. "I'm not afraid of you, Nichols. I wasn't when you drenched me at Matt's pool party when I was eighteen. I'm not now."

He frowned. Oh hell, he hadn't thought of that day in years. Who was he kidding? His subconscious pulled it out from time to time. Her brother had thrown an eighteenth birthday party. The whole team had gone. He'd started to come out of the haze of despair that had become his constant companion by then. He still didn't know how he'd had any friends at that point. That second party had been the only time Cole had spoken to her after that kiss that had changed everything.

She had refused to get in the water. Because he hadn't known how to talk to her or apologize, he'd looped one arm around her waist and carried her in. In the water, he'd wanted to talk, to explain. To hold her.

But she'd been angrier than a half-drenched kitten.

"You sure about that, Jamison? I seem to recall you didn't like me carrying you in. You probably don't want all that popcorn in your hair."

She narrowed her dark eyes. "Who says I'm the one going to end up with popcorn in my hair?"

He smirked. He liked that about her. Even when she was outmatched, she didn't give—

Another piece of popcorn hit him on the nose and she was off, running around the island.

She was going to pay. He caught her easily enough and she laughed and squirmed while tossing pieces at him.

He grabbed a handful and pulled back her sweater, dropping them inside.

"Oh no, Cole, really?" She squealed as she laughed.

He grinned. "You asked for it." Three hours with her and he was playing. When was the last time he'd played?

She might have protested, but she was still reaching for the pieces that had fallen on the floor and then she tossed them as she ran.

Again she didn't get far; he picked her up easily with one arm. She squirmed and he said, "Easy does it. Trucc? I don't want you to hurt yourself." He put her back down.

Her chin jutted up. *Me?* I'm not—"

It hadn't been his intention to kiss her. But she was

wrapped in his arms with her eyes dancing and, well, damn it. It seemed like a good idea at the time. And she tasted like freaking heaven. Sweet, with just a hint of spice. And just one brush of his lips did him in.

Synapses in his brain fired the danger alert code. But the nerve endings in his body fired the "keep doing this" code. He kept the kiss light. Just a tiny taste. Just a little something for Christmas to make him still believe in wishes. Even though he knew better.

But then everything changed. Instead of pulling back with a shocked or concerned expression, she mewled, and then looped her arms around his neck. She was pressing her body into his and she was kissing him back.

Cole slid a hand down her back and pressed her against his body. *Yes. Hell yes.*

Even if this was a dream, it was one he could get behind. He'd sleep half the damn day if it meant more kisses like this.

Her tongue danced with his, tangling and twisting. Forcing his to chase hers. In a flash, he picked her up again and she wound her legs around his hips.

He couldn't breathe; the desire contracted his lungs and airflow. With much effort, his brain made a few feeble attempts to come back online.

Jamie worked her fingers over his scalp and he groaned in ecstasy. It might not have been smart, but he didn't care. He needed to stop thinking and right now she was the panacea he needed.

She tasted familiar yet illicit at the same time. In a matter of seconds they were seventeen again in Frank's house, playing seven minutes in heaven.

The second she'd touched her lips to his, he felt like someone had poured gasoline on him and lit a match.

And none of that feeling had gone away. In fact, it was worse. *Much, much* worse.

A flood of endorphins rushed through his blood as he remembered everything about that night seven years ago in startling clarity. From the taste of her lip balm, to the feel of her soft skin. And somehow it was more potent now, more visceral. He couldn't get enough and he wondered if it might be possible to explode from a kiss.

Cole slid his hands under her sweater and around her back, relishing her velvety skin. She felt like satin under his fingertips. Her soft sigh like a balm to his soul.

Bringing his hands back to her torso, he skimmed her ribs. Tracing each with his thumbs. When his thumbs rubbed the soft undersides of her breasts, Jamie gasped and arched into the caress.

She threw her head back, breaking their kiss, and he smiled to himself as he watched her. She wanted more. She was wound just as tightly as he was. Just like him, she remembered.

He needed more. Needed to touch her, hold her.

With a frustrated growl, he snatched up the hem of her sweater. "Let's toss this, shall we?"

She nodded absently and reached for him. He was more than happy to oblige, surpassing all thought that told him this was a bad idea.

He dragged that hideous sweater over her head and tossed it aside. "There, that's better."

She blinked into focus and grinned. "Yeah, it got really hot in here. Wonder why."

She was so damn cute. "What do you say we get rid of this too. Make you more comfortable?" He tugged on her Cyberpunked T-shirt. Wait, what the hell? He frowned and focused on three lines of code with colorful, punk rock, rainbow font. *Cyberpunked.* "Where did you get this T-shirt?"

She looked down. "Oh, I had them screened and printed for all the employees. You know as a team-bonding thing. What, you want one?"

Cole's gut fisted. *Oh hell.* He gently lifted her away from him. Jamison Reed was J.L. Reed. The one woman he couldn't make comply. "You want to explain why the hell you won't sell to me?"

She frowned, then blinked.

It took her a second to process. But he could tell when it finally dawned on her what he was asking. She stumbled back as if she was on fire. "You're Teched?"

Cole crossed his arms. "Yeah. Want to answer my question?"

This was the man trying to take everything from her. She knew the vultures were circling and his company was the biggest, baddest bird among them. They didn't think Cyberpunked could withstand the tide. Well, she'd just have to prove him wrong.

She glared up at him, then drew herself up to full height. "The only way you're coming near me, or my company, is over my dead body."

He glowered at her. "That can be arranged." He'd spent the past half day with her. How was he just finding this out?

"I'd like to see you try."

Chapter 6

It wasn't exactly like Jamie was avoiding Cole. It only *looked* like avoidance. So what if she'd locked herself into the guest room and worked all day? That was what she had planned for this little staycation anyway.

It had absolutely nothing to do with the gyrating make-out session yesterday. *Nothing.* Okay, maybe a *little* something. But she didn't have a clue what to say. Or do. After that little mutual revelation, she hadn't even said a word, just walked upstairs and locked herself in, only surfacing for breakfast and to reset the router. And breakfast had been a hurried standing-up affair while she shoved a muffin into her mouth and hoped he didn't see her hiding in the kitchen.

She didn't need to explore the grounds. Or enjoy the fireplace. Or the Christmas tree she'd decorated. She was perfectly fine in her room working.

She wasn't hiding at all. *Pants on fire.*

She wasn't at all concerned that she was living with the enemy. Rooming with the one man who wanted to rip apart her life. No, wait, considering Brandon, make that the second man. Jamie kept trying to tell herself it made no difference now that she knew who was behind Teched. The same rules applied. Work her butt off, get the game done and live to fight another day.

Her phone rang and she rummaged through her laptop bag to dig it out. She answered with a grin when she saw who was calling. "Hey, Mia. How is the newlywed? Shouldn't you be holed up in some fabulous location with your very sexy husband?"

Mia Donovan had grown up in Hope, just one town over from where Jamison and Cole had grown up. She and Mia had often competed in the debate tournament together. She was one of the few friends Jamie had kept from high school.

Her friend laughed. "Oh, don't you worry, Ryan and I are getting plenty of *alone* time. It's been a little hectic trying to start the production of my new show as he drags me halfway around the world on my honeymoon for three months." Her friend was the producer of a weekly docuseries for the TVN network.

"Oh, the woes of a woman in love," laughed Jamie.

"I know you said you were going to be in town, and Ryan surprised me with a trip home to New York for the holiday. I'd love to see you if you're around."

A chance to see Mia, *and* get the hell away from Cole, she was so down for that. "I would love to see you. Do you mind meeting me halfway in say, Reynolds? They have that pub on the edge of town. It's a bit hipsterized but might still be fun."

A night out was just what she needed. She'd been working all day and was making good progress. A few hours to give her brain a rest weren't going to kill the time line.

"You're on. Seven thirty?"

"Sounds perfect." She hung up the phone with Mia and finished the component she was testing. Tonight would be good. When she got out of the house and away, she would be able to find her calm, rational center.

At seven that night, she came down the stairs to find Cole sitting in the living room. Just her luck, she'd been hoping that he was maybe working out or something.

He looked up with a start and stared at her. "Where are you going like that? There is nothing to that dress."

She looked down at her dress. Okay, so maybe it was a little low-cut, showing off her cleavage, but it wasn't so bad. And she had on the black tights, thick enough they may as well have been leggings, and ankle boots. "What's your problem?"

But she wasn't an idiot. She knew what his problem was. Given the way his eyes roved over her body and the way her skin prickled from being the focus of his complete attention, she knew his thoughts were likely on yesterday.

A frown marred his smooth forehead and she could guess he was also thinking about how she was never going to give him what he wanted. He wanted a piece of her and her company. And she would rather walk into the blistering cold, stark naked, than let him have it…*or* her.

She had spent the last ten months hating this man, despising everything he stood for. Just her dumb luck that she wanted him.

They glared at each other, locked in the other's gaze for several moments before he finally spoke. "Nothing."

She skipped down the remainder of the stairs. "For your information, this is a dress. I'm sure your last girlfriend wore far less than this all the time. I'm dressed appropriately. Now, if you don't mind, I'm going out."

His brows remained furrowed. "Where?"

She grabbed her purse off the coffee table and tossed in her phone, then turned around slowly to face him. His slow sweep over her body made every single one of her nerve endings crackle and pop under the zinging electricity of his stare. She spoke slowly and deliberately, making sure to enunciate. "Out. I have a key—I'll be fine."

"The snow is coming down pretty hard out there. Are you sure you should go out?"

"I know this must be confusing for you, but I have a father *and* a brother. Neither one of whom are here at the moment. And even if they were, I'm an adult. I can go where I want, dressed how I like. I don't need you breathing down my neck. The weather is fine." Actually, she'd seen the fluffy flakes and opted to cab it instead of drive herself.

He crossed his arms. "Jesus, Jamison. The roads are a mess right now."

She sighed. "It's Jamie. I know you think you're being protective or whatever, but let me remind you, you are not my brother."

His gaze flickered to her breasts before he dragged it back up again to meet hers. "I think that's pretty clear."

"No, you're just the guy trying to take away my life." She hitched her thumb toward the door. "I worked my butt off all day trying to keep my company afloat. Now I'm going to go and have a drink with a friend. I'll see you when I see you."

Her phone buzzed, presumably indicating that her

ride was there. She quickly pulled the phone out of her purse to verify the caller, then dropped it back in as she stalked into the mudroom to grab her long coat. She didn't bother with the second glance backward.

It took Cole exactly five minutes from the time Jamison left until the time he dragged on his shoes and followed behind. Sure, he could tell himself all kinds of things.

Like, he was worried about her. The snow had really started to accumulate. He also told himself that he wanted to go after her to hash out their Cyberpunked and Teched problem. That one was his favorite lie.

Even though a bar was probably the wrong place for that conversation. And oh yeah, he was frustrated. *Really, really* frustrated.

But the truth was, he'd seen her come down the stairs and he'd forgotten all about Cyberpunked or the way she was thwarting his acquisition. Kept forgetting that for the better part of the last year she'd deliberately aggravated and confused him.

No, all Cole cared about at this point was that he wanted her. All day, he'd been trying to think of something to say. An excuse to go up and talk to her. And it had nothing to do with his attempted acquisition of her floundering company.

Cole was in trouble. *Bad* trouble. Because, instead of enjoying the solitude he said he wanted, he was chasing after some sassy-mouthed girl who wouldn't listen to him about what was best for her. All because she kissed like a dream. *Don't go there. There is no going back.* Even thinking about her lips was enough to bring back memories he didn't want.

But that didn't stop him from going after her. He'd

known without her telling him exactly where she was going. And there wasn't much out here, except for the pub in Reynolds.

Twenty minutes later, when he walked in, he tried to keep his head down. The pub screamed old English pub with the dark oak interior, hearth. It also went the extra step showing Premier League football on the mounted television screen in the corner. And the aroma of Scotch eggs and bangers and mash made his stomach rumble.

"Hey, Cole. Good to see you back. What'll it be?" asked the bartender. Jack? John? His name was something like that.

"Just a Seven and Seven."

"Coming right up."

When his drink arrived, Cole nursed it and watched the basketball game on the sixty-inch monitor until something hit his foot. He peered down at the white cue ball and shook his head. Someone must have been getting a lesson.

A pretty girl with mocha skin, a wide smile and the most unusual blue eyes Cole had ever seen jogged over. "Shit, I'm so sorry. I have no idea how to play pool. My friend decided it might be a good idea to teach me. I think I'm making her regret that decision."

Cole laughed as he shook his head. "It's no problem. She's probably just forgotten what it was like when she learned."

She grinned. "Why don't you join us? I'll even buy you a drink to apologize for assaulting your foot with the pool ball."

He glanced over at the pool tables and saw a telltale streak of green hair and didn't have to think twice about that. "I'd love to join you."

When he approached, Jamie's eyes went wide and

then she scowled. That look right there was totally worth his coming out. "What are you doing here?"

Man, did he like getting under her skin. "I was accepting your friend's gracious invitation to come play with you guys." He introduced himself properly to Mia and her husband, Ryan. "Jamison's staying out at my parents' place for the holiday."

Mia's gaze flickered to her friend and back to Cole. "Jamison, huh? You should've brought Cole along. The more the merrier. Christmas spirit and all."

Jamie did her best to ignore him and shifted so she stood on the other side of Ryan. "Cole's not really big on Christmas spirit," she muttered.

He watched as she lined up her shot but missed, then a very inventive curse spilled out of her lips that made him proud. So he was getting to her.

The Jamison he used to know never would've cursed. The innocence had practically dripped off her. Not anymore though.

Ryan nodded at his half-empty glass. "The least we can do, Christmas spirit or not, is buy you a drink."

Cole shook his head. "No. I'm good. Besides, you saved me from drinking alone all night, so I'm buying."

One of the waitresses scooted by and he ordered a repeat of what everyone was drinking, but Jamie changed her order to a tequila shot, and then glowered at him when he looked askance. Oh really? She wanted to go down that path?

"You know what? I'll change mine to a tequila shot too."

It would only take him an hour before regretting that decision. Four tequila shots in and he was concerned he was actually getting drunk. He knew Jamie was already there, or tipsy at least.

Mia and Ryan were a fun couple and obviously in love. He liked them a lot. But Mia became his favorite person of all time when she nudged him and pointed out that Jamie was standing under some strategically placed mistletoe in the corner.

"I think maybe you might know how to cheer her up." She grinned before adding, loud enough for Jamie to hear, "Now, if you don't mind, I'm going to go dance with my husband."

He approached Jamie carefully. She was still mad at him. But she looked adorable standing under the mistletoe, completely unaware of her position. "What about you—do you want to dance?"

"With you? Somehow, I don't think that's in my best interest."

He had to laugh. "You're probably right about that. But how about it? It's just one dance."

Her gaze slid around. "I'm not really a great dancer."

That was a lie. He'd seen her dancing plenty of times. She just didn't want to dance with *him*. He reached for her and took her hand. "One dance, Jamie. Call a truce and it's one dance. And you don't even have to leave your spot. No one is watching you here in the corner."

She stared at his hand for a moment, then lifted her gaze up to meet his. With a sigh she let him pull her into his body. "Fine. If it makes you go away. Just one."

He nodded and pulled her against him, relishing how they fit together. "How about for a little while we just forget everything."

"Sounds like a plan to me. I'd love to forget that you're trying to steal my company."

Cole pressed a finger to her lips and shushed her. "Ah, you promised." And then because he was feeling mischievous, he pointed up. "Did you come stand over here on purpose?"

Her head tipped up and she groaned. "You knew I was standing under it?"

His lips lifted into a smile. "In my defense, it was Mia who pointed it out."

"Traitor. She thinks everyone else should be in love just because she is."

Cole smiled at her. "Isn't it bad luck or something if we don't kiss? Given your unholy obsession with Christmas, you'd think you'd know this."

Damn, he shouldn't have had that last shot. If he'd been 100 percent sober, he'd know that kissing her again was the path to disaster. He'd know that he wouldn't recover from it. He'd know that neither of them would thank him in the morning.

But he didn't care. Since she'd left him downstairs yesterday, he hadn't been able to think about anything else. His brain had flickered between past and present. They were long overdue for a civil conversation, but he doubted they could handle being courteous. He'd loitered in the living room and the kitchen for the sole purpose of catching a glimpse of her. He'd even kept the fire lit all day in an attempt to tempt her to come down. But she hadn't. There was no way he was passing up an opportunity to kiss her now.

She swallowed and licked her lips. "I might take my chances with the bad luck. I don't like you. I certainly don't want to kiss you again. Matter of fact, your balls might be in danger if you do it again."

Cole leaned over her, his heart thundering against his ribs. "One kiss, Jamison. Prove to me it was a fluke. Convince me that we definitely don't want to go there again… I'll be plagued by the same dreams I had for the rest of senior year."

She pulled back and narrowed her gaze. "You acted like I had the plague…after…you know."

He ducked his head. "Jamison, I—"

She interrupted. "This is a bad idea for so many reasons."

He focused on her lips as she spoke and he tried to make his brain work. *Good luck with that.* He swayed them gently to the music. The Weeknd played in the background, but he could barely make out the lyrics. "You think I don't know that?"

She licked her lips. "Of all the lodges in all the world…"

He chuckled low under his breath. "You had to walk into mine."

"You can't have Cyberpunked." Her chin lifted so she met his gaze.

"Right now, all I'm thinking about is you."

"I don't believe you."

"Jamison?"

"Yeah, Cole?"

"Then I'll just prove it to you and kiss you again."

He pulled her farther into the shadows where they'd be obscured from view. Her lips parted in invitation, and he immediately forgot where they were. He didn't care. The only thing that mattered was how she tasted and felt and how desperate he'd been since yesterday to touch her again.

She moaned as she wound her arms around his neck and slid her hands into the hair at his nape. Cole took full advantage, deepening the kiss, wasting no time trying to get his fill.

The problem with kissing Jamie was, there *was no*

getting his fill. The more he did it, the more he wanted to do it again. He wanted to spend hours exploring every single inch of her body. He wanted to hear his name on her lips.

Lifting her, he deposited her on a nearby stool and relished her sweet taste as he licked her mouth. Why was she the one to make him feel like this?

He should stop. *They* should stop. But he couldn't find a reason to give a damn right now. All he could see was her. All he wanted was her. From somewhere behind them, someone whistled low and muttered, "Wish someone would kiss me like that."

That dragged him back into consciousness and he pulled back. Jamie moaned at the loss of contact. "We should go."

She nodded slowly trying to bring herself back to focus. "Yeah, okay, let me just say goodbye to Ryan and Mia."

This is a bad idea. He didn't care. *In the morning you'll regret everything.*

Screw the morning. Maybe if he had her once he'd be able to exorcise her from his head. He'd be able to focus again.

The chilly night air clung to them in the cab as they huddled together. The scent of her apple shampoo wafted into his nostrils. He tightened his arm around her and her heat seeped into his skin, warming him from the inside out. As the snow fell, it stuck together in fluffy clumps.

The whole cab ride neither said a word. He just held her close as he tried to think of any way this could be a good idea. When they pulled up to the house though, it wasn't a hot night that awaited them. Jamison was fast asleep. He'd known there was no way she'd be able to handle all those shots. Laughing quietly to himself, he carefully picked her up and carried her inside the suite.

Her coat and shoes were a challenge. She kept wanting to curl up into a ball. "Oh no you don't. You can't sleep in your shoes, princess."

Even though he almost got a foot to the face for his efforts. Apparently, she was ticklish. But he couldn't help the smile that tugged at his lips when he noticed her tights were decorated with mistletoe and reindeer. She really went all out. Wow, these were so damn hot. Her feet were delicate in her thin thermal socks.

With the glow of the Christmas tree lights illuminating the room, he lifted her against him and tugged her coat off next. She murmured something then rolled into the couch. "Up we go." She was so small in his arms as he carried her up the stairs. His body might not believe it, but maybe this was better. They were on opposite sides. And she was right. He did want everything she'd built. *Because she's brilliant.* Somehow in the middle of fighting, he'd forgotten to tell her that.

Chapter 7

Harsh sunlight streaked across Jamie's face and she yanked the blanket over her eyes.

Uh-oh. Fast jerky movements were not so good. A heard of elephants had taken up residence in her skull. One of them knew how to work a jackhammer. *Crap.* She was hungover.

In a breath, it all came crashing down on her. Dinner and drinks with Mia and Ryan. Playing pool. Drinking tequila shots. Fighting with Cole. *Kissing* Cole. Always Cole. Damn him.

As foggy as her brain was, she remembered every single thing about the dancing *and* the way he'd kissed her under the mistletoe. Unless she'd imagined all of that? No, she remembered the distinct taste of him. A mix of tequila and mint and *him.*

There had been kissing…lots of kissing and…her mind went slightly fuzzy after the kissing.

No, wait, she also remembered rising heat and need mixed with the fear of what he stood for. There had been fighting, hurled accusations. She remembered the cab. Or rather climbing into the cab, and having his scent linger around her, his heat wrapping around her like a cocoon, keeping her warm. Then…nothing.

Panic flooded her veins. There was a reason why she rarely drank. What had she said? What had she *done*? Tequila was the devil. What was that song by T-Pain? Except she couldn't blame it on the alcohol.

She'd *wanted* Cole to kiss her—she'd been wound tight since he rescued her from the stool. Who was she kidding? Ever since she'd seen him again she'd wanted to see if she'd imagined that night back in high school.

A quick glance around told her she was in her bed. On the nightstand sat a bottle of aspirin and a glass of water. Taking it nice and easy, Jamie forced herself into a sitting position, trying to see if any nausea would accompany the rocking headache.

No. She was in luck today. Sort of. Her dress though, was all twisted around and stretched out. *Damn.* Maybe she could get it to keep its shape if she dry-cleaned it.

After a hot shower and a change of clothes, she felt marginally better. At least more human, and not like a tequila-soaked cotton ball. This week was already off to a hell of a start. Maybe it was worth considering leaving early, before she did something really stupid…like make out with Cole again.

But it was Christmas season. So another place to stay would be hard to come by. Cole might not be the ideal companion, but he was better than nothing. Even if he was a pain in the ass. A *sexy* pain in the ass… Who wanted her company.

It didn't matter how he made her feel. He'd have to pry Cyberpunked out of her cold, dead hands.

Firing up her laptop, she frowned. The data transfer should be done by now. Why was it taking so long? On the top right corner of her screen, there was an icon that told her why. The network signal strength was slow. Good thing she came prepared for everything. The weather might be the cause. She'd brought a signal booster in anticipation. Except, where did she put it? It wasn't in her bag. Probably in the car. With a glance out the window, she groaned. It was really coming down. The last thing she wanted to do was go outside…or, let's face it. See Cole. But she'd have to see him sooner or later. She'd just hoped for *much* later.

She tugged on another Christmas sweater and headed downstairs to face the music. The scent of bacon met her as soon as she opened the door.

She found Cole in the kitchen in front of the frying pan turning a piece. Whoa. She was not equipped for situations like this. Awkward. Morning afters were not in her repertoire. She cleared her throat before saying, "I thought you didn't cook."

Cole turned and smiled at her. "Look who's awakened from the dead."

Jamie winced. "Must you shout?"

His answer was a grin so hot she suddenly remembered why she had been drinking tequila. He increased his volume. "Who's shouting?" Jamie groaned and he laughed. "Sorry. Sorry. Can you do me a favor and grab two plates. Breakfast is served. Oh, and I put a glass of water and some aspirin on your bedside table. Did you take one?"

"Yeah, thank you for that. I feel better than when I woke up."

"How bad is it? Head and stomach or just head?"

She winced and eased down onto one of the stools. "Isn't the head enough?"

"Well, let that be a lesson to you before you start sucking down tequila like Tijuana was your birthplace."

"Why aren't you hurting? It's not fair."

The corners of his lips teased up into a lopsided smile. "First, I'm bigger than you are, so I can drink more. Second, this is not my first trip to the tequila road show, and finally, I drank a large glass of water last night. I would have offered you one, but you were dead to the world."

Probably not her finest moment. "Thanks for tucking me in." She cleared her throat. Time to pay the piper. "Uh, I remember us kissing, but not much after that."

His brow furrowed and he planted his hands on the counter. "Is there a question in there?"

"I just don't remember what I might have said...or done."

His brow lifted. "So you don't remember threatening me with bodily harm or the added fun of wiping out my future descendants if I ever kissed you again?"

She flushed but muttered, "It's not my fault you drive me to violence."

They both spoke at once. "Look—"

"About what happened—"

She sighed. "Go ahead."

He nodded. "I shouldn't have kissed you. Clearly, it's some residual curiosity thing from high school. No big deal. We'll just forget it."

She stared at him as the heat of embarrassment made her skin prickle. *Residual curiosity.* If he'd said that to her last night, no wonder she'd threatened to maim him.

She might not remember much, but *something* had happened between them. She'd felt it.

"Seriously? That's what you're going with? I'm trying to be a grown-up here, and you want to go with that route. You know what, you're right, that was a mistake. Clearly, the tequila talking."

She turned on her heel, but he was in front of her in a flash. "Geez, Jamison—"

The fury that had been simmering boiled over. "It's freaking Jamie. I hate being called Jamison," she shouted. "You think I don't know what you were doing last night? You really think kissing me would change my mind?"

His eyes went wide. "Fine. *Jamie*, do you want to tell me why you're so pissed off at me? All I'm trying to do is bail you out. Why don't you just bend? You have a perfectly good offer on the table. But instead, you're fighting like hell toward a deadline you have no hope of making."

"You know it's a good thing that kiss was such a damn mistake. Just like our first kiss. Because I'd be furious if I thought otherwise. I could never be interested in someone who knew so little about me. I'm fighting because that place is *everything* to me. Those employees count on me. I built Cyberpunked from the ground up and you want to dismantle it. It's my soul."

His voice went low and he took a step toward her. Every nerve ending on her body went on red alert. The tension rolling thick around them like fog so dense not even fog lights could penetrate. "I *know* you, Jamison. I've been studying your games for months, finding the angle, understanding your brain. You're damn brilliant, but you're hurting yourself and your company by not taking the out. You don't take my deal, somebody bigger and meaner is going to come along."

"You don't know anything about me." She wished she at least had on shoes so he didn't dwarf her. "You want to take something from me. Something I built. With my bare hands, with my heart. And the worst part is you claim to understand me but you can't even see how you not believing I can pull off that game says the opposite. *I* believe in miracles. I believe in myself. Why would I ever sell Cyberpunked to someone who doesn't have faith in me?"

He ran his hands through his hair. "Oh, I have faith in you. Your mind is brilliant, complex and nuanced. I want someone like that on my team. You think I got to be where I am with Teched without recognizing good talent? You're the one who doesn't have the best judgment. I mean, come on, a guy like Brandon? How could you not see him for what he was? He's not as good as you are and it's apparent in the work he puts out. But you." He threw up his hands. "You just let him walk away with half of your company. I mean come on."

Jamison glared at him for a moment. "Tell me something, Cole, why do you want Cyberpunked so bad? You've been after me for months. Is it maybe because I'm the first person to ever tell you no?"

He blinked and truth flickered in his eyes. "Don't be ridiculous."

"Oh, I think it is. No one has ever told you no. Sure, you've walked away from lots of people, but no one has done the same to you and it irritates you."

His gaze narrowed. "Is that what's really bugging you? That I walked away from you? Geez, Jamison. Oh, excuse me, *Jamie*. Way to hold a grudge. I was—"

She put up a hand and cut him off. "No. We are not

doing this. You're wrong. And I'm done. I'm going to get my signal booster out of the car. Let's do each other a favor and keep a wide berth for the next week. Now, if you'll excuse me, I need my booster."

His brow snapped down. "What? Now? It's nearly a blizzard out there and the garage is down the hill. Don't be ridiculous."

"I have work to do. I can't move forward without it, so I'm going."

"At least wait till it lets up a little."

"You'd like that, wouldn't you? If I missed my deadline."

His shoulders stiffened. "I don't want you to fail. I want—"

"You know what? Doesn't matter." She wasn't listening to any more. She was tired and behind schedule.

As the tears pricked at her eyes, she blinked them away. Crying wouldn't solve anything. She grabbed her coat from the mudroom and wrapped her scarf around her neck. Barricaded against the chill as much as she could, she winced when a gust of wind slapped her in the face. Hell, that was cold. Chin down, she pressed on, even as the snow whipped and whirled around her. Her feet made crunching noises in the soft-packed snow as she walked. Every step required Herculean effort. But while the snow was coming down, unlike last night, it wasn't sticking. It was too dry in the air for that.

The garage was just down the hill. But why did it seem like a mile away? *Suck it up.* She needed that signal booster if she was going to get this game done.

At the locked garage, she pulled out her keys. She fumbled with the door, the keys in her hand, and dropped them on the ground. Just as she fished them out of the snow, a gust of wind hit her in the face on an inhale.

For a very long moment, she couldn't breathe. The pain in her lungs started first before spreading outward into her chest with each shiver.

She gasped and tried to suck in another gulp, but nothing. Then the panic set in. *No. Relax. You know better, stay calm, stay focused. Slow steady in, slow steady out.* But she couldn't remember her breathing exercises and the panic made it worse.

Something was coming up behind her, but she was too cold to turn around.

"Damn it. You are so damn stubborn. Come on. I'll get the damn booster."

"N-no."

"Just stop, Jamie, you're going to get sick. You have asthma. It's dangerous for you to be out here."

He remembered that? "I need to finish."

He had to scream over the howling roar of wind. "Not today you don't. If you need it so bad, I will get it for you. Come in or I swear to God I will carry you."

He wouldn't. But one glance at the firm set of his lips and she knew that he wasn't playing. He'd only tossed on his peacoat and scarf. He hadn't even properly laced his boots when he'd come out after her. *Idiot.*

With a growl, he bent down and picked her up. "You're struggling to breathe. So shut it."

Son of a gun. Her world spun for a moment as Cole scooped her up, cradling her against his chest... Too tired to fight, she went limp as he carried her back to the house.

As soon as they were inside, in the warm air, she felt better. Her breathing was still shallow but easier.

He carried her into the massive living room and left

her on the couch to run upstairs. When he came back, he had her inhaler and thrust it into her hands. "Use this." Cole's beautiful mouth was set in a firm hard line as he tugged off her boots and coat.

She opened her mouth to protest that she might not need it, but he glared at her. "Now, Jamie, I'm not playing with you."

"Cole, I—"

He held up a hand. "No. You're going to use this, then you're going to rest. After that, you and I, we're going to talk. But right now, you need to relax, use your damn inhaler and drink some tea. And I don't want any attitude."

Well, attitude was her middle name. But right now, she didn't have any fight in her. *Later.* She'd fight him later.

Chapter 8

Cole paced the length of the living room as he watched Jamison sleep. *Oh, excuse me. Jamie.* The fear still mixed with anger in his blood. The tightening in his chest hadn't dissipated even though he knew she was okay. She'd gone out in that weather to prove a point. He admired her tenacity, but she was too stubborn for her own good.

He'd tried to work, tried to focus on something else, but no. All he could think about was her. She'd barely eaten any of the soup he made her, insisting she wasn't hungry, but he knew she had to eat. She had drunk the tea though, so that was a step in the right direction.

The moment he tried to relax he would think about the reason she was out in the snow. Because she was stubbornly trying to hold on. *Or, maybe because you threatened to take her company from her and she doesn't want to lose.* He wanted Cyberpunked. Almost as much as he wanted her. If she just stepped back she'd see he was right. But this wasn't about that. She'd been trying to prove something. To him, to herself.

He'd seen it in her face when she said she was used to people not believing in her. There had to be a common ground somewhere. Because they couldn't do this for the rest of the week.

They'd both been on edge for the last two days and she'd gone running headfirst into a snowstorm with her asthma. He'd nearly lost his mind when he saw her, dressed to head out into the cold. Everything they weren't talking about was getting in the way. *Put up or shut up, Nichols.* If he cared about her, they needed to clear the air.

She stirred on the couch and he stepped to her side. "Do you need anything?"

Dark eyes slowly blinked into focus. "No. Honestly, Cole. I'm fine. You've been hovering for hours."

"What am I supposed to do? You triggered an asthma attack heading out into that weather. You didn't even have a hat on. What were you thinking?"

"If you're going to scream at me, then I'm going to go up to my room."

"I'm not—" He modulated his voice. "*See*, I'm not screaming. But you could have gotten really sick. What if I hadn't come to get you? Was that booster worth your health?"

She squeezed her eyes shut. "Oh my God. I needed it to get my work done. And, yes, I know. It was stupid. It won't happen again."

"You're damn right it won't happen again. At least not on my watch. You try a dumb stunt like that again and I'll handcuff you to the couch or the bed or something."

"You didn't strike me as the kinky sort. But hey, no judgment."

Despite his annoyance, his blood hummed. This woman was infuriating, stubborn, a pain in his ass. But she was also beautiful, intelligent and creative. And she had the one thing he wanted. Well, two. Sure, he wanted Cyberpunked, but he wanted her too, wanted her on his team. He wanted her in his bed. "You get that I'm serious right? You can't go back out there. I'm trying to look out for you."

"Because you want Cyberbunked."

"I'm not trying to take care of you because I want your company in my portfolio. I'm trying to take care of you because I haven't been able to get you out of my damn head since I was eighteen."

Her eyes went wide. "But—"

Cole licked his lips. "I know. But I—" Screw it. He was done doing what he was supposed to do. He leaned down close and her lips parted on a sigh.

His lips ghosted over hers and he was lost.

Jamie parted her lips and sank into his embrace. His tongue licking into her mouth. He relished the way his body tingled, the adrenaline jolt to his heart, the way his body hummed. It was like she was his personal defibrillator.

When he pulled back slightly, she whimpered and tried to tug him back. He sucked in a deep breath trying to find his equilibrium. It was like trying to grasp air.

"Cole?" Her voice was breathy and soft, like the whisper of satin on his skin.

His lips tipped into a smile. "I see you still wear that strawberry lip balm." He touched his forehead to hers. "I know neither of us has brought it up yet, but we should probably talk about our first kiss and what happened after."

His heart hammered against his ribs and he watched her carefully. He didn't like talking about it. Hell, he never talked about it. Not even with his mother. But they were locked in the house together. Jamie pushed herself into a sitting position. It was hard getting used to calling her that. He'd always used her full name as a way to poke at her. *Time to deal directly, Nichols.*

"I love that we've both been dancing around the elephant in the room, pretending it's not eating the popcorn off the Christmas tree and lounging on the couch with us." She laughed.

Damn, this was harder than he thought. But if he wanted to be on some kind of even ground with her, they needed to have this conversation. "First, I know I acted like an ass. And I want to say I'm sorry."

Jamie wrapped her arms around her knees and tucked her feet under the blanket. When she spoke, her voice was barely above a whisper. "Can you tell me what happened? I didn't think it was me alone. I mean, you withdrew from everything. You skipped that sports season. Hell, you even stepped out of the running for valedictorian. It's a hollow win when no one is pushing you." Cole smirked at her competitive streak breaking through. "I just wanted to help or something." She shrugged. "I could tell something was bothering you, but you wouldn't talk to me."

He nodded. "After that party was winter break. My Dad and I had this big Christmas blowout party planned. Dad loved the holiday. Everything about it. Gave turkeys to the homeless and also bought the most ridiculous presents. He was the first one to wake us up on Christmas morning to have us open our presents.

Dressed as Santa, the whole thing." He inhaled deeply. "That year we went out to Idaho to see my uncle. There was an accident on their way back from getting the tree. He died."

"Oh my God, Cole." She reached out and took his hand.

The warmth of it spread through him. "Dad was driving and from what the police said, they'd hit a patch of ice and couldn't control the car." He drew in a shuddering breath. "My mom handled everything with a startling efficiency. All the funeral arrangements were made in Idaho. Most of Dad's family was still there. Within a couple of weeks, we were back home, memorial had and I was back at school. I didn't get much time to grieve or even let it sink in. It was like Mom couldn't deal with the sadness so she tucked it away and thought I should too. But I couldn't. Looking back, I know I was depressed. I didn't care about school or sports or my friends anymore. I just shoved all my feelings away." He shrugged. "Anyway, I've never been one for the holiday since then. Too painful to think of how much he loved it and what a cold empty thing it was after he was gone. Mom tried, but it was obviously never the same. It was missing the zest and sparkle."

"Shoot," she muttered. "And here I am with all my holiday cheer and sweaters, and eggnog and tree. I'm totally insensitive. I wish you'd put your foot down and told me you didn't want it."

He shook his head. "The thing is, it was kind of nice. You're the only person I've ever met who loved the holiday as much as he did."

"Yeah, but still, the last thing I wanted to do was make it more difficult for you." She ran her hands through her hair and pushed the oversize sweater sleeves up her slender arms. "I'm sorry."

"Don't be. Despite my mood, it's been…nice. So thank you. It's the first time someone has been hell-bent on making me enjoy it. Asthma attacks notwithstanding." He licked his lips. "I, at the very least, owed you an explanation."

"Cole, you didn't have to let me do all this."

"I did. Having you here reminds me of how much I miss it and how much of an effort I need to put in to remember this. Remember him."

"So you're telling me you want an ugly Christmas sweater," she said, obviously trying to diffuse some of the tension swirling around them.

"You know what, I'll pass."

Cole brushed a strand of green hair off her cheek. "I'm happy you're here and I can't seem to stop kissing you because I think you're sexy and smart and I can't *not* touch you anymore. So I'm just going to focus on that for a minute."

Jamie nodded slowly. "I can get behind that."

His chocolate-brown eyes focused on hers. "I was thinking we call a truce on work talk. Maybe take the day off and do something fun. We can resume fighting the day after Christmas. Besides, a tiny elf once told me, Christmas is meant to be enjoyed. Not hidden from."

Jamie sagged into Cole's arms… A truce. She could live with that. And she wanted this. Yearned to be with him. For a few more days, she could exist in this fantasy before she had to face the real world.

Her breath hitched as he used one hand to wind around her back and draw her close, while the other skimmed up her ribcage and teased the underside of her breast. A moan escaped her lips before she could stop it.

"Your skin is so soft. I used to wonder how soft you'd be right here." He nuzzled just behind her ear.

"Cole—" Jamison's head swam. The delicious tingling making her feel weak all over.

"Focus on my voice. Just feel."

She could do that. She wanted to be with him. Pretend that he could be hers just a little bit longer.

Cole bent his knees, then picked her up gently. He carried her down the long hallway to his bedroom. When he laid her down on his bed, she reached for him, pulling him to her.

The only sound that filled the room was their hushed kisses, muffled moans and rustling clothes. As the fire crackled they kissed, touched, explored.

Her sweater went first. Then his Henley.

Piece by piece, they stripped away layers of cotton and wool; she tore down her outer emotional walls brick by brick, allowing herself to really feel. To relish every touch and emotion.

Voice shaking, his hushed whispers filled the silence. "You're killing me, Jamie…so damn pretty." When she ran her teeth over his earlobe, he swore softly.

He knew exactly how to get her where he wanted with his hands, his tongue. When he placed openmouthed kisses down her jaw and along her throat, her head swam.

As he sucked, she wound her hands in his hair, tugging gently, leading him. "Cole, please."

He was driving her crazy. Did he want her to beg? In a tangle of arms and legs, bare flesh slid against bare flesh. When Cole finally rocked into her, his skin against hers, her only thought was *So this is how it's supposed to feel.*

Chapter 9

Cole woke with a start, something snapping him out of the dead stupor of sleep. Which was unusual, because he normally didn't sleep that deeply. He was always thinking and too busy planning. His brain never seemed to take a rest. Like he was on a perpetual hamster wheel where someone kept ratcheting the dial up.

But last night he'd slept. His restlessness was one of the main reasons he didn't have many sleepovers. Even with Clarissa, whenever she stayed at his place he slept like crap. Even the slightest movement was enough to wake him. But given the filtered streaks of sunlight, it was morning, so obviously he'd slept.

Next to him, Jamie snuggled into his side and he smiled at her bare back. Last night's death-like slumber was more than likely attributed to the workout Jamie had given him. For the first time in a long time, all he wanted to do was stay here and watch her sleep. Usually, he was jumping out of bed to exercise or to make a call. To stay ahead of the curve. Get in front of the pack. To have others chase him. But he was content to just hang out.

He liked her in his arms. They might bicker when they were awake, but in bed, it was easy. *Too easy.* Holding her last night was like grasping a shooting star when he never thought he could accomplish such a deed.

Jamie was soft and silky all over. The apple shampoo she favored blended well with whatever mixed-spice lotion she used. He'd seen the bottle in her bathroom. Autumn harvest or something.

Little Jamie Reed. She wasn't so little anymore. How long had he fantasized about touching her, holding her? *Years.* And she was his. *Only for a moment.* It wasn't permanent. He'd do well to remember that. Her butt wiggled against him once again and he had to smile. She was probably seeking warmth, but if she kept moving like that…yup. There it was. The blood from his brain flowed straight to his erection, not caring about rational thoughts like that he'd kept her up late, making love until she'd passed out asleep on top of him. She needed sleep. But maybe, just maybe, she needed him too. He kissed her shoulder and she breathed deep, snuggling again.

Last night might have been a fluke. But now that he'd had her, he wanted her again. As many times as he could manage before they had to leave and return back to their lives. He wanted her in his bed. *All* the time. That wasn't actually a bad idea. He should keep her in bed. Outlaw clothing altogether for the rest of the holiday.

Cole's erection nudged her ass and he groaned when she shifted her butt, cradling the length of him. Was she awake? Aware that she was torturing him? Conscious of what he wanted from her? Or was she just minding her own business getting some rest after a long night? Cole was just enough of a jerk not to care. If he only had a limited amount of time with her, then he wanted to be with her as much as possible. He smoothed her hair away from the nape of her neck and kissed her softly.

That got her attention because she moaned deeply. She turned in his arms with a sleepy smile. He might not love the holidays now, but she reminded him of everything he'd loved about the holiday as a kid. With her color-streaked hair on his pillow and smile on her face, she looked resplendent. She was so sweet. When she stretched, the motion forced his focus to her soft mounds.

In his defense, they were pressed right up against him. How was he not supposed to stare? Or salivate. Or itch to touch, tease, taste. He wasn't made out of stone. With his eyes still on her breasts, picturing the fun they could have in the shower, it was her posture that clued him in that she was less than thrilled. Forcing his gaze to meet hers, he asked, "You okay? I didn't keep you up too long, did I?" He should feel bad that he'd been trying to wake her for the last hour or so…but he didn't.

She blinked her dark eyes into focus and stared up at him. Her mouth opened, then she closed it again. She repeated the motion several times before she started speaking. "Uh—no, I slept fine. Thanks." She tried to gather the sheet around herself and sit up, but he stayed her hands.

"Hey, where are you off to in such a rush?"

"I should go. You know, shower. All that kind of stuff. I'll just—get out of your hair." Cole brushed his thumb over her knuckles. As a by-product, her sheet slipped and he was momentarily distracted by her breasts again, but he was able to hold it together a little better.

"Stop. I don't want you to go. Besides, we're in your room."

Her brow furrowed. "Uh, right. It's not a bother. I… don't usually do…" Her voice trailed.

He offered helpfully, "Sleepovers?"

A shy smile crept over her lips. "Never actually. I… sort of have no idea on etiquette. So maybe it's just better if I go and leave you to it. Or you go…whatever."

He shook his head. "You must not have listened very well when I told you I don't want to go." He leaned forward and placed a testing kiss on her lips. She didn't pull back so, him being him, he took a little advantage and kissed her deeper. He waited until she moaned low before pulling back, his breathing more choppy and uneven.

She looked like it was a struggle to keep her eyes open, but when she managed to focus, she asked, "You are very good at that. And *really* brilliant at distraction. But what happens now?"

"Well, now, we kiss some more, because I'm becoming an addict. It's better than coffee to get me going in the morning."

She swatted his wandering hands. "You know what I mean."

He did. "Well, the way I figure it, we have a history. And we're obviously good together. *Better* than good."

He nuzzled the hollow behind her ear and her breath hitched. He wanted her almost as badly as if he hadn't already had her…several times. Cole forced himself to take a deep breath. This was important. If he wasn't careful he could spook her. "I think we get in trouble when we talk about work."

She was about to protest, but he held up a hand.

"Hear me out. For good reason. I understand your position even if I don't agree with it. We're both passionate about it. You came here to work and so did I. Neither one of us knew that we'd be here together. And given our past, it could be awkward, but I think that if we don't venture into that terrain, we'll be okay."

She chewed her lip. "We can't spend the next week just being naked with each other."

"I'm inclined to disagree, but I know what you mean. You're worried we'd need to talk about something."

She nodded, sending her multicolored hair swinging around her shoulders.

"As much as I've maybe forgotten, and you too, we are more than our jobs. We have interests in other things. We can talk about that. I am actually curious about what you've been up to all this time. I want to know where you've traveled. I remember you had this whole map thing and when you went anywhere you pinned it."

Her smile was bright. "I can't believe you remember all of that."

Little did she know. "I remember everything about you. The way you always wore your hair, the different colors you had. That strawberry-bubblegum flavor of your lips. I haven't forgotten anything. The way you used to laugh and talk trash when you were beating your brother at Halo."

Jamie shook her head. "How do you remember that?"

"I may have been half zombie then, but, once I had a taste, you kept sneaking under my skin. You were everything that I wanted. I used to watch you out of the corners of my eyes. Every party. Every class. You were on my mind."

Chapter 10

This was a dream. A fantasy that was going to end. *So enjoy it now.*

They'd spent half the morning in bed. And Jamison felt…delicious. Her muscles were pliant and…exhausted. She tried not to focus on the dark spot of gloom looming just over the horizon. That they were on opposite ends of a dividing line. Or that in a few days, after the holidays, they'd go back to their lives and she'd be alone…again.

No. Now she was going to focus on the fun. For once. Eventually, when Cole had finally let her out of bed, she'd called the family in France to wish them a happy holiday. Cole had made her breakfast in bed, then they'd embarked on their epic Christmas adventure. Ice skating, followed by a horse-and-buggy ride and now this.

She stood at the top of the snow-covered hill and frowned at Cole.

"I'm not sure about this."

He grinned like the children who surrounded them,

with their squeals and peals of laughter. "You can do this. Come on. We'll go down together." He held up the tandem sled. He looked relaxed and happy. As if that young, carefree Cole was back.

"Do you even know if that thing is safe?"

"Of course it's safe. It'll be fine."

She'd done this as a kid, but she'd been terrified every time. Much like now. "You know. You should just go ahead. I'll just wait in the lodge."

He laughed. "Come on. Where's that girl who used to challenge everything? Let's do this." He slid his gaze away. "It's okay if you're scared."

Yes. She was. But she didn't need him to know that. "Give me the damn sled."

He laughed as he handed it over. "God, you're easy."

"Shut up." She dropped it on the fluffy snow. "Are you getting on or not?"

"Yes, but only because you asked so nicely."

The kids around them were far more devil-may-care. Never mind that it was a fifty-foot slide to the bottom. And that they could break all manner of bone going so fast. They were gleeful in their abandon. She, however, was older so she knew to be afraid.

Cole climbed in behind her and he wrapped one arm around her waist. "Go on, Jamie. It's now or never. Time to let go."

She inched them close to the tipping point and she dragged in a deep breath. *Oh God. Oh God. Oh God. Go go go go go.* With one final glance back at him, she tilted them over the edge.

This was fun. Cole was having a blast. At a time of year he normally dreaded, he was out and about having a great time. Because of Jamie.

Next to him, in the car, she sang "Jingle Bell Rock" at the top of her lungs. He didn't even mind that she was tone-deaf. *Completely.* When they passed the turn for the house, she stopped.

"Where are we going?"

"You'll see. Are you forever trying to ruin presents? I thought you liked surprises?"

"I do." She grinned. "I also like to figure out a mystery. Don't ask questions. I'm a woman. That's just how it goes."

"Why is that always the answer women give? That doesn't explain anything."

"Then you will forever be relegated to not understanding us at all."

She resumed her singing for the rest of the drive and when it came to the last song, he even joined in at the end.

When they pulled in to the cabin her mouth dropped open. "Oh, no way!"

He laughed. "Yes way." When he was a kid, his father used to bring him and his brother up to the one-room cabin to leave presents for Santa and the elves, and wrap presents for their mom. He'd called ahead and had it cleaned out, decorated and a fire started. It had been seven years since he'd been out here.

The caretaker had been more than happy to deck out the cabin in all things Christmas. White Christmas lights adorned the smaller trees leading up the path to the front door. Two snowmen, complete with carrot noses and scarves, welcomed them onto the path for the front door. Through the glass wall of the living room, he could see the fire in the massive fireplace.

Jamie did a little dance when she walked in. "My God, it's beautiful."

He nodded. "My dad used to bring me up here. I haven't been here since he died. It's bittersweet. It doesn't hurt as much as I thought it would."

He'd been specific. There needed to be a massive tree with all the decorations, and stockings with their initials as well as gingerbread cookies just like when he was a kid.

The enormous cabin was open-plan with a loft feel. The massive king-size bed against the far wall. When he was a kid, there had been bunk beds. Everything from the mostly modern decor, to the floor-to-ceiling glass wall, to the marble fireplace and the softer-than-sin, faux-fur rug taking up all the room on the floor between the couch and the fireplace screamed opulence.

"This is perfect. Thank you."

His smile for her was automatic, but then it usually was. "You're welcome."

In the kitchen champagne sat on ice on the kitchen table, as did a full spread of chocolate-dipped strawberries, cheese and fruit. And just like he'd requested, a large flask of hot chocolate awaited them.

The timing was perfect. He'd given the caretakers a thirty-minute window and they'd gotten everything ready just in time.

The more he thought about it, the more he realized a girl like Clarissa was never going to want to come somewhere like this.

"Geez, you really know how to woo a girl."

When they settled in front of the fire he shook his head. "Nah, just *this* girl."

She frowned. "It's unsettling how well you know me."

Cole shrugged. He wasn't telling her how much he'd

wanted her. How attuned he'd been to her. "Not really. Lucky guess."

"Cole…" She cleared her throat. "I got you something. I know how much you loved mine, so…" She pulled the gift box out of the bag she'd brought and handed it to him with a wide smile.

Warmth spread through his chest. He'd been given lots of presents in his life, but this one from Jamie made his heart squeeze. He didn't want to examine the well of feelings too closely. The moment he had the lid off, he started laughing and couldn't stop. She'd bought him a sweater with a his and hers Rudolph kissing on the front. It was perfect. "I love it."

She laughed with him. "That's right. Join me in the ugly-sweater loving. Welcome to the Christmas side. Get it? Instead of dark side?"

He pulled her forward for a kiss, his lips gently brushing hers. He wanted to hold on to his moment forever.

He pulled back though, not wanting to get too distracted. He had something for her. He tugged a tiny package out of his pocket. "I, uh." He swallowed. "I, uh, ordered this the other day. I was lucky the store does delivery at Christmas. It's just a little thing. But it seemed perfect."

Tears welled in her eyes as she reached out and took the delicate chain. "Oh my God. It's beautiful." The tiny globe, studded with diamonds, shimmered in the firelight. "I can't believe you're giving this to me. It's too much."

He shook his head. "It's perfect. Thanks to you. I'm enjoying my first Christmas in years. So, Merry Christmas."

Her eyes shimmered as she gave him a kiss. In just a few days, he'd have to let go of her. The only problem was, now, he didn't think he could.

Chapter 11

Even though Jamison knew this wasn't real, she couldn't help but feel happy, and relaxed. She still had a lot of work to do in a short amount of time, but somehow felt energized even though she was taking a whole day off to play.

When Cole pulled back into the long driveway leading up to the lodge, he stopped the car and took her hand, smiling. "You look pretty with that necklace."

They'd made a pact. This was the rule that he'd set. But a part of her wanted his opinion. She wanted him to see how good she was. Maybe if he saw, he'd back off.

She wanted him to see that she was working her ass off. To see how important this company was to her.

And that was the fundamental problem. He *didn't* see. He might care about her, but he still didn't respect the work she had done or could do. She took her hand back and slid it into her lap.

When she reached for the door, his voice was soft.

"Jamie, come on. Let's hold on to today for a little longer."

"I don't think I can. Playing hooky can be fun, but the truth is, I can't afford to pretend for long."

Once in the suite, he tugged off his jacket. "I'm sorry. You think I'm trying to destroy your company. That's not my intention."

She threw her hands up. "Why can't you see that? While it's not your intention, it's what you're still doing."

"And why—" He cut himself off.

She flung her scarf onto the nearest hook. "Why what?" She shook her head. "Why have I worked for the company that I built with my bare hands? If it were your company, you wouldn't be asking that question. You'd be fighting with your last breath. If I were a guy, you wouldn't question my determination at all. You wouldn't question my ability."

"I don't question your brains, Jamie. Hell, you're probably smarter than I am. But you're clearly killing yourself. You're smart. You're super creative. It's crazy actually. But your business is struggling. And I think, maybe, it wouldn't hurt to have someone who knows how to run a company in charge. There's nothing wrong with your brain—there's something wrong with your level of experience."

She could feel it, the switch go off in her head, the trigger for total detonation. "My level of experience? I'll have you know I ran the company successfully for the last four years. *I* am the reason the company is still tugging along. We may be in a challenging situation, but we're still alive. That last game? That did really well in the market. That was *me*. I oversaw everything from design implementation, to Q&A. It was *my b*aby."

"And that's exactly my point. You should have more people who oversee all that. You can't do *everything*."

"I would love to have people. You think I don't want that? I'm just guilty of falling in love with the wrong person. Not making him sign the noncompete clause. That was my mistake. My *only* mistake. You think he's doing well right now? Nope. He can't get his head out of his ass and realize that it's not about ego but about producing the best game. And his clients are suffering for it. They'll be back. I just need to be around to receive them."

He shook his head. "You're delusional, if you think they'll return. In the meantime, you're working yourself to the bone. I've been watching you. When you work, you barely eat. You don't sleep. How do you think you're going to survive until they magically show up? You can't have it all. We can amend the terms of the sale. You stay on as the creator, you own the product, we just trim the fat a little bit."

She threw her hands up. "You're not listening. The company is *mine*. I'm not going to let someone step in, dismantle it and get rid of my staff, or as you say, 'trim the fat.' I need every single person on my team. I know how to select talent. You just see a bottom line. You're no better than a corporate headhunter. Yeah, you might know about building your company, but you sacrifice the people who love what they do."

"You don't know me."

"Are you happy? Cole? Are you? Because you don't look like you have any joy. You look tired, and stressed, and you barely laugh. If that's what it's like to be part of what you're assembling, then I'm not interested."

She might care about him but she couldn't fathom

handing over everything she'd worked for. Especially to someone who was going to rip it apart.

His lips set in a grim line. "I may not seem content to you, but I'm creating a legacy. You're working toward a pie-in-the-sky dream. If you really had a business head, you'd see that you need the courage to change. You need it *and* you need the money. I'm offering you a way to get it. I want you on my team—I'm not trying to get rid of you."

"You don't understand, Cole. I *am* Cyberpunked. You dismantle that company, you dismantle me."

"And that's exactly my point. You aren't that company. You are *you*. You're a creator, a designer, a coder. But I don't think you can run a company and I'm offering to help you."

She stared at him. That's what he thought he was doing? He thought he was helping her? He didn't think she could do it. Just like Brandon. They'd argued bitterly about the company direction. He hadn't believed she knew what was best either. This was her dream and she was going to see it through. "You know, the past couple of days have been fun. Like a dream. But I'm not going to concede defeat. Not to you. Not to anyone. I'm not selling to you. I'm not letting you take my employees. I'm not allowing you to dismiss my company. I will fight you till the bitter end. *I. Am. The. CEO.* And I know how to make my company thrive. This thing with us? It was incredible, but clearly a mistake."

"Jamison, would you just stop and listen for a minute. I want to help you. But you're being stubborn. We can work this out. Let's come to a mutually beneficial agreement. It doesn't have to be like this."

She walked into the suite quietly and could feel the heat of his gaze on her back. Determination in her posture. She didn't have time to fight. She had work to do.

Chapter 12

So close. Almost there. Jamison could almost taste the victory. She'd only found three major bugs. One of their developers back in the city had already fixed one and was checking to make sure he hadn't introduced new bugs. That left two remaining issues and she was almost through with the game. She just needed another day. Not that she really had that kind of time.

When a game was finished, she ran through it and tried to determine the glitches, then she sent it out to beta testers, comprised of a couple of reviewers, bloggers and some die-hard fans. They would be brutally honest, but she was appreciative of the feedback and would offer them an advance copy as compensation. It was important that it went well. The reviewers and bloggers were all respected in the industry and if the game didn't deliver to expectations or there were fundamental flaws, they'd roast her on a spit in the reviews.

After they sent in comments, it would ship out for final testing and packaging. So this was the time to cross her fingers. If she could finish this round tonight and test out the fixes and their components tomorrow, then she'd be home free. This close to saving Cyberpunked.

The knock at her door was soft. Cole *again*. Butterflies fluttered low in her belly as her body instantly warmed to his presence. Unfortunately, the longing was also accompanied by wariness. "Come in."

He opened the door, brandishing a to-go mug of coffee. "I thought you could use this."

Sweet. He could be so sweet. Unfortunately, he could also be an ass. She still didn't understand why he could be so considerate one moment and at the same time have zero faith in her. From her position in the beanbag chair in the corner, she said, "Thanks. I appreciate it."

When he handed her the cup, their fingertips brushed, but he didn't linger. "I was thinking you could use some food too. You've been up here for a few hours. The last thing I remember you eating was the yogurt I dropped off at lunch time."

"I appreciate the concern, but I don't really have time to eat right now."

"Make time, Jamison."

She frowned. Back to Jamison, huh? He'd called her Jamie for two days. She liked it better when he called her Jamie. "We've been through this. I'm really close. I just need one more day. Just see if there is a granola bar in the kitchen or something."

He crossed his arms and pressed his lips together. "No. You need to eat. I'm ordering food—I want you to come down. And while you're at it, why don't you take a break, a nice hot shower, change of clothes. You've been holed up in here for two days since we arrived back from the cabin."

He might have had a point about the shower. Her room was a disarray of candy wrappers and papers and her notebooks. So many damn notebooks with all her little notes. She didn't want to miss anything. Cleanliness was nothing on her priority list right now. She winced when she thought about the state of her hair.

"I'll be down in a few minutes."

He shoved his hands into his pockets and rocked backward. "I'm not trying to be a pain in the ass, but you said that hours ago. I'm just trying to look out for you."

"Real food, a shower, it can all wait. I just need one more day and I'm done."

He ran his hands through his hair and mumbled something.

"What was that?" she asked.

"Nothing."

She levered herself up onto her knees. "No, you obviously have something to say. A continuation from the other day maybe?"

"Fine, I'll say it. You're wasting your time. You're good and I want you to be happy, but you're not going to make it. You can't be the CEO of your own company like this. You're a mess right now and I admire the passion, but you're killing yourself for this one game, this one Hail Mary. It's ridiculous. You and I both know how this is going to go. And even if you managed to pull off your Christmas miracle, the investor will probably back out because of your lack of experience, the history of the company, something. Some arbitrary reason. All that work and you have a way out. Come on, just take it."

"You know, you sound just like Brandon. He said I'd be under within months. I've lasted over a year."

His handsome features morphed into a scowl. "You're seriously comparing me to that asshole again? You really thin—" His phone rang.

Jamison tipped her head up to meet his gaze. "You're about to get that."

"Jamison, we're not done."

"Yeah, we are."

With a curse, he dragged the phone out of his pocket. "What?" He listened for a moment, then turned his attention to her. "Listen, give me a few, I need to take this."

She watched him go, then glanced back at her laptop. They *were* done. Thinking she could pretend with him would only get her hurt and she had a greater responsibility than that. It was time to go home. She could stop in Hope, spend the night with Mia and Ryan, then head for the city in the morning.

She'd tried to get away from it all. She'd tried to find her miracle. Maybe Cole was right and there were no such things. Only hard work and determination were going to get her through, and she was almost there.

She couldn't stay. It was time to face the real world. With tears in her eyes, she backed up her drives and packed her bags and laptop. She could leave the rest, including the possibility of loving Cole. She didn't need it anymore.

Chapter 13

Irritation rolled off Cole in waves. Damn it. That whole conversation took a lot longer than it should have. Instead of a quick ten-minute chat about the numbers and the dates of one of the properties they were trying to acquire, it took a damn hour. At least now he could talk to Jamie in peace.

Cole walked out into the great room and checked the kitchen. "Jamie, where are you?" There was no answer. Had she gone to the lodge? At the foot of the stairs, he called up again, "Jamie?" The panic set in as he hit the midway point on the stairs and realized that the house was empty. Not just quiet, but *silent*. For the last several days since they put up the tree, the moment Jamie woke up, she plugged in the musical Christmas lights.

She was also prone to play music when she worked. The last couple of days he could tell how well everything was going by what music she played. If it was flowing well, she played the Johns, Legend or Mayer. If things were going *really* well, she played old-school Sean Paul.

If she was feeling irritated with a section, she would play some hard-core rock like Nine Inch Nails. Not too loud but there was extra noise. Right now, there was silence.

His heart hammered against his ribs. She'd left. He didn't bother knocking at her door. Instead, he barged in. She wasn't there. Neither was her stuff. She'd left one of her sweaters with her Christmas gear. But otherwise, she was gone. He couldn't believe it. He ran to the other master. But before he even went in, he knew what he would find—nothing. No Jamie, no laptops, no servers, no hardware. *Empty.* The last hour he'd been on the phone in the study, she had quietly packed up and snuck off into the night.

For the next two days of Cole's stay, he worked like a man possessed. Christmas had come and gone, so everyone should at least be by their phones. So much for giving his workers some time off.

He called Jake, even though he knew the guy had three kids under the age of six at home. As soon as Jake answered the phone, his words were terse. "Where are we with Cyberpunked?"

His friend sighed. "Look, Cole, I get it, but it's several days after Christmas and not a lot of people are working now. I put some things in place to find out what we can do about their potential investor, if you're sure you want to sweeten the deal for them to invest in Cyberpunked, but you have to know you are the only one working right now."

Truth. Everyone in the world was getting ready for

the new year. He understood. Hell, if they hadn't had the stupid fight, he and Jamie probably would be taking time off once she finished.

But no, she'd left him. It wasn't so much that she left, but that he started to wonder if being with her was a possibility. That hurt the worst.

The cabin was empty without her. He shook his head trying to shake the shadow of her from his mind. "I don't give a damn. I want you to find someone who can answer my questions. And then I want you to go find that investor, offer them anything to invest. Promise them a partnership if you must."

Jake sighed. "We've had this argument. I'll do what I can. But you need to consider a plan B. You might not get what you want this time."

Jake's words clinked around in his head like a rusty bench. Jamie. She was what he wanted. He hadn't been this happy or relaxed in a long time. Because of her. And he not only wanted her in his bed, but he wanted her in his life. He needed her to see that she needed him. And he'd pushed her away. *I. Am. An. Idiot.*

He rubbed at the sore spot in the middle of his chest. He'd gone from being overworked and overstressed just a few days ago, to relaxed and happy, and now back to a frustrated workaholic in a matter of days. He'd screwed up. "Just find that investor." He hung up on Jake before his friend had a chance to respond. He knew he was being a jerk. But he had to do something to get her back.

As he stewed, he thought of what Jamie had said about loving what she did. That she just needed an infusion of cash. He thought of what Jake just asked. What made her so special? What made her unique was her determination. Even in the face of certain failure, she was going out swinging. And that deserved his respect. She reminded him of his father.

On his laptop he did a quick search of her name. Maybe it was time to look at things differently. He loved her. Maybe it was time to show her that.

Chapter 14

So this was what failure tasted like. Jamie shut down her laptop and sat back in her chair, whirling around to look out at the New York City skyline. The game was done. She worked all through the Christmas season. She did exactly what she'd said she was going to do.

Only to find out today that she was going to lose it all anyway.

The investor was backing out. After everything, they'd gotten cold feet. The finalized game was releasing tomorrow, a few weeks ahead of schedule. But they wouldn't see game proceeds for at least another quarter. She was screwed. She was going to have to tell everybody who was busy working their butts off out there that it was over.

With a sigh she picked up the phone to call her lawyer and figure out how best to handle giving the employees whatever cash they had left. He answered on the second ring. "Hi Mark, it's Jamie."

"Jamie, I was just about to call you."

"I know. I just heard from Terry. I tried everything I could. And I still failed. I can't believe some guy just swooped in and made the deal go away. They said they had a better, more lucrative deal somewhere else. I don't know where. This deal has been in the works for months." Cole had been right. Maybe she did need to sell.

She could hear Mark's chair squeak on the other end of the line. "Wait, you haven't heard?"

"Heard what?"

"I told Brianna, my assistant, to contact you about thirty minutes ago. To tell you not to do anything drastic. We've got another offer."

She sat up abruptly, nearly tipping over her chair. "What do you mean another offer?" Someone else wanted to buy her company? Someone else wanted to give her the cash she needed? Two different options. Did she dare hope?

"I don't know anything about them. I have their holding company name and I've had researchers trying to follow the rabbit hole, but maybe you'd be able to find something. You are the genius hacker computer type. They want to invest."

Sweat rolled down her back. Could this be real?

"Yeah, give me the name. Obviously I want to find out everything I can."

"Suite Investments. Ever heard of them?"

No, she hadn't. "No, but give me a couple hours. What's the offer?" They had time to do due diligence. "In the meantime, I'll need to take out a loan to hold us till then." He gave her the figure and she whistled low. "What's the catch?"

"As far as I can tell, all they want is a repayment of

a quarter of the amount within a year, and then the remainder of the amount invested to be donated to charity for underprivileged children over the course of ten years."

"But that's crazy. What do they get out of it?" By now she'd learned that if something sounded too good to be true, then it was.

"They only ask that you spend a quarter of your time working on special incubator projects for them."

"We have to find out who they are."

"You get to work on your end and we'll figure it out."

She hung up on him and pulled her laptop onto her thighs then leaned back to look out the window as she typed.

If she did this, she'd get to keep her company. And most important, she'd get to keep the place running until the profits rolled in for this game. She could prove that she was capable of doing this. With money like that, she had time. This was the miracle she'd been asking for. But somehow, it felt hollow.

After three hours of unraveling complicated financial filings and pretty decent security parameters, Jamie glared at the name on her screen. She knew who wanted to invest. She just didn't believe it.

Cole had done this. After everything, he'd been responsible. He backed off the other company. But why? And why would he hide it?

He made it perfectly clear last week that he didn't believe in her. They needed to talk. And not just because she was dying to see him. She would only see him to sort this out. That was all. Not like she hadn't been able to sleep for days without him.

Like a masochist, she'd driven by his office, sort of

hoping for a glimpse of him. But she'd only done that once because, honestly, how pathetic could she be?

He'd been so clear. The little voice in the back of her head screamed that it wasn't a good idea. *You will only get hurt this way.* She didn't feel like listening. She felt like answers.

It took her less than twenty minutes to drive from her office in Williamsburg to Teched. But when she arrived there, she couldn't pull the trigger. All she could do was sit in her car for another ten minutes getting up the nerve to do what she had to.

Could she face him? After running? Both of them would've said something that they couldn't take back if she'd stayed. Mostly, she'd been afraid that just like Brandon, he would take everything she had to give and leave her with nothing.

But he's not Brandon. Did he have faith in her? She wanted to believe that. But what she wanted to believe and the truth were sometimes two very different things. With a deep breath, she finally found the courage to brave the blustering winds and run to the door.

The vibe at Teched was completely different than Cyberpunked. The building was monochrome and steel, all white and gray palate. There was no joy, no happy, comfortable feelings. This was corporate. And it was cold. And she didn't want any part of it.

Although, she'd take the money. She had employees to pay. But she wanted to know why. Why was he doing this after everything he said to her? When she walked to the front desk, a pretty brunette smiled at her.

"You must be Jamison Reed."

She frowned. She'd been expected?

"Jamie Reed, yes. Is Cole available?"

"Yes, we've been expecting you. Please wait here for just a moment."

Jamie didn't bother taking a seat in the uncomfortable-looking slanted chairs. If she got a satisfying answer from Cole, she'd have to talk to him about his decor.

The pretty brunette came back. "He's waiting for you down the hall, in the conference room to the left."

Waiting for her? Which meant he knew she'd come looking for him. There was nothing she hated more than being a foregone conclusion.

Never mind. She despised being broke more than she hated that. So for the sake of her company, and her friends, she could deal with him.

She opened the door to the conference room, and was immediately struck by the color. Vibrant and happy, the walls were painted a pale yellow, the chairs and loungers were bright shades of red and green and orange. It looked like a meadow had exploded in here.

Cole was in one of the loungers and staring at the enormous monitor on the wall. When he saw her, he stood, looking just as sexy and mouthwatering as he had a week ago. Damn him.

She didn't want him to be sexy. She didn't want to want him. *Well, too bad for you. Now get your question answered and get out.*

"I see you got my bread crumbs." He smiled.

She didn't want to still feel the pull of the attraction to him. But reality was far different. It was very nice to desire things, but she couldn't always get what she wanted. "You didn't make it particularly easy to follow but yeah, I found you."

"I knew you wouldn't respect the offer if I didn't challenge you."

"Why do all this, Cole? You pretty much said you

didn't think I had the guts to do it. To be the CEO of my company. To see everything to the end. So why would you invest in me? That makes no sense."

"You ran away. I turned around, and you were gone."

As he moved closer, she backed up a step. Her skin felt tight and itchy and she wanted to relieve the sensation by rubbing herself all over him. *Focus, Jamie.* "There was nothing left to say. You ran off a perfectly good investor. Someone who believed in me. Someone who I was about to show what I could do, and you ruined that." He shoved his hands in his pockets and rolled back on his heels.

"At the beginning I was an idiot. I didn't run off your investor. I actually tried to sweeten the deal for them to invest in Cyberpunked. I knew you wouldn't take money from me and I wanted you to have your dream. Every day since you left, I've been replaying that conversation in my head. And each time I think, why didn't I say it differently? Why didn't I just tell you that I hated seeing you work yourself to death like that? Why didn't I just tell you that before I knew you were Cyberpunked, I wanted the brains behind the company? But after I knew you were Cyberpunked, I pursued the company *because* of you. I want you because you can see the future. Once I knew that person was you, it seemed inevitable."

"Cole—"

"Not inevitable," he interrupted. "I just didn't know that you could be the dreamer, and be the hardheaded businessperson too. I was wrong."

She tipped her head up and stared at him. "I don't need you to be sorry or wrong. I need this, but I can't take your money. I won't."

"I knew you'd find out I was behind it. Frankly, I

thought it would take less time. I expected you this morning. I was so caught up in what I wanted and what I had to have. I believe in you. You're the kind of person I would back. I don't need to be in control. This is your show."

She opened her mouth to say something but she couldn't find the words and shut it again. With a deep breath she tried again. "Why?"

"Damn it, Jamie, why don't you see that I'm trying to tell you that I love you?"

Oh. That wasn't what she was expecting at all. "I am—"

"You don't have to say anything. I couldn't get you out of my head for years, then I had you within grasp and I screwed up. Seeing you again was a rapid free fall. And next thing I knew you were gone. Those few days were the happiest I've been in a long time. That day in the cabin. When we just drank hot chocolate and talked? That's probably my favorite day of the last seven years."

Jamie's breath came in and hitched to gulps. She loved him. She'd always loved him. "So at the cabin, when you gave me the necklace?"

"I guess I didn't know it then, but I was asking for a real chance. What we had that day was genuine. And I know it was a short amount of time. And I know that we don't really know each other anymore, but I wanted to show you that I did believe in you."

Jamie gently fingered the necklace underneath her turtleneck. She hadn't taken it off.

"Cole, I *need* this money. But it has to come from someone else. I can't take it from you."

He took a deliberate step toward her, his eyes pleading.

"Jamie, I know. It's the only way I can think of to say sorry. The terms stand. It's a loan. Not a gift. You would give me a quarter of the amount in a year's time, the rest to charity." Well, that's something he would do. He always believed in investing in people, and not necessarily the business but the *person*. "And I believe in you. I'm not like Brandon."

Her brain tried desperately to filter through everything he said. All she caught was the main focus points. He loved her. He believed in her. That's all she'd ever wanted from someone. "I shouldn't have left like that. I know how it feels."

He leaned toward her, closing the gap between them. "I felt like my heart was being ripped out when I realized you were gone. I never wanted to feel like that again."

"I love you. And…I'm sorry. I freaked out because I was hurt and I needed to get away. It reminded me of Brandon and the way he treated me. Like I wasn't important. Like he was the important one, the one with all the great ideas."

He cursed low under his breath. "I didn't mean it like that. I was just frustrated. I do believe in you. And I would like to help you. Not take over. But business aside, if you tell me no, that's fine. I will help find another investor to keep your doors open. It's you I want. I no longer want to acquire the company."

Jamie blinked away happy tears. "You're serious right now?"

He nodded.

"Then I want you."

He pulled her close. "I love you. I've always loved you. And I always will. And most of all, I admire your unwavering optimism. Your full, wholehearted love of Christmas and ugly sweaters. Your adoration of all things red and green. Eggnog and cinnamon, Christmas carols. Your lovely smile. And I love how hard you work. And I love your heart and how you care for people."

"I'm so lucky—I received *two* Christmas miracles. My company and most important of all, you."

* * * * *

To my in-laws, Bobby and Petrina Lister, for keeping the
magic of love alive for more than fifty years.

Acknowledgments

My Heavenly Father, thank You for my life.

To my husband, Lance, my children, family and friends—
thank you for your continued support.
I appreciate and love you!

A special thank-you to the readers and authors I've met
on this journey. You continue to enrich my life.

Thank you to my editor, Patience Bloom,
for your editorial guidance and support.

A very special thank-you to my agent, Sarah E. Younger.
I appreciate you more than words can say.

Dear Reader,

Christmas is my favorite holiday of the year, with family,
fun, food and of course all the spectacular desserts! I love
creating appetizers and bite-size desserts, and had a blast
"researching" all the ways to incorporate chocolate in this
book for my heroine, Maya Brooks. She's at the top of her
game, but not really feeling the holiday spirit. Then again,
neither is Ian Jeffries. But there is just something in the air at
Christmastime that can affect the most reluctant of hearts. I
hope you enjoy Ian and Maya's journey to finding that magic
called love.

Thank you for all of your emails and messages. I love hearing
from you!

Wishing you all a beautiful and blessed holiday season.

Much love,

Sheryl

Website: www.sheryllister.com
Email: sheryllister@gmail.com
Facebook: Author Sheryl Lister

YOUR PARTICIPATION IS REQUESTED!

Dear Reader,

Since you are a lover of our books – we would like to get to know you!

Inside you will find a short Reader's Survey. Sharing your answers with us will help our editorial staff understand who you are and what activities you enjoy.

To thank you for your participation, we would like to send you 2 books and 2 gifts – **ABSOLUTELY FREE!**

Enjoy your gifts with our appreciation,

Pam Powers

**SEE INSIDE
FOR READER'S
SURVEY**

For Your Reading Pleasure...

FREE!

We'll send you 2 books and 2 gifts
ABSOLUTELY FREE
just for completing our Reader's Survey!

YOURS FREE!
*We'll send you two fabulous surprise
gifts absolutely FREE, just for trying
our books!*

Visit us at:
www.ReaderService.com

YOUR READER'S SURVEY
"THANK YOU" FREE GIFTS INCLUDE:
▶ 2 FREE books
▶ 2 lovely surprise gifts

▶ DETACH AND MAIL CARD TODAY! ▶

PLEASE FILL IN THE CIRCLES COMPLETELY TO RESPOND

1) What type of fiction books do you enjoy reading? (Check all that apply)
○ Suspense/Thrillers ○ Action/Adventure ○ Modern-day Romances
○ Historical Romance ○ Humour ○ Paranormal Romance

2) What attracted you most to the last fiction book you purchased on impulse?
○ The Title   ○ The Cover   ○ The Author   ○ The Story

3) What is usually the greatest influencer when you <u>plan</u> to buy a book?
○ Advertising   ○ Referral   ○ Book Review

4) How often do you access the internet?
○ Daily ○ Weekly ○ Monthly ○ Rarely or never.

5) How many NEW paperback fiction novels have you purchased in the past 3 months?
○ 0 - 2   ○ 3 - 6   ○ 7 or more

YES! I have completed the Reader's Survey. Please send me
the 2 FREE books and 2 FREE gifts (gifts are worth about $10) for which I qualify. I understand that I am under no obligation to purchase any books, as explained on the back of this card.

168 XDL GJ3D/368 XDL GJ3E

FIRST NAME	LAST NAME

ADDRESS

APT.#	CITY

STATE/PROV.	ZIP/POSTAL CODE

Offer limited to one per household and not applicable to series that subscriber is currently receiving.
Your Privacy—The Reader Service is committed to protecting your privacy. Our Privacy Policy is available online at www.ReaderService.com or upon request from the Reader Service. We make a portion of our mailing list available to reputable third parties that offer products we believe may interest you. If you prefer that we not exchange your name with third parties, or if you wish to clarify or modify your communication preferences, please visit us at www.ReaderService.com/consumerschoice or write to us at Reader Service Preference Service, P.O. Box 9062, Buffalo NY 14240-9062. Include your complete name and address.

K-216-SUR16

© 2015 ENTERPRISES LIMITED
® and ™ are trademarks owned and used by the trademark owner and/or its licensee. Printed in the U.S.A.

READER SERVICE—**Here's how it works:**

Accepting your 2 free Kimani™ Romance books and 2 free gifts (gifts valued at approximately $10.00) places you under no obligation to buy anything. You may keep the books and gifts and return the shipping statement marked "cancel." If you do not cancel, about a month later we'll send you 4 additional books and bill you just $5.44 each in the U.S. or 5.99 each in Canada. That is a savings of at least 16% off the cover price. It's quite a bargain! Shipping and handling is just 50¢ per book in the U.S. and 75¢ per book in Canada.* You may cancel at any time, but if you choose to continue, every month we'll send you 4 more books, which you may either purchase at the discount price or return to us and cancel your subscription. *Terms and prices subject to change without notice. Prices do not include applicable taxes. Sales tax applicable in N.Y. Canadian residents will be charged applicable taxes. Offer not valid in Quebec. Books received may not be as shown. All orders subject to approval. Credit or debit balances in a customer's account(s) may be offset by any other outstanding balance owed by or to the customer. Please allow 4 to 6 weeks for delivery. Offer available while quantities last.

If offer card is missing write to: Reader Service, P.O. Box 1867, Buffalo, NY 14240-1867 or visit www.ReaderService.com ▲

BUSINESS REPLY MAIL
FIRST-CLASS MAIL   PERMIT NO. 717   BUFFALO, NY

POSTAGE WILL BE PAID BY ADDRESSEE

READER SERVICE
PO BOX 1867
BUFFALO NY 14240-9952

NO POSTAGE
NECESSARY
IF MAILED
IN THE
UNITED STATES

BE MINE FOR CHRISTMAS

Sheryl Lister

Chapter 1

Maya Brooks rolled her eyes as the woman on the phone went on and on. "Yes, Mrs. Harper. I know I told you the shop would be closed the last three weeks in December, but my plans have changed and I'll be able to provide the desserts for your party if you haven't found someone else."

"That would be lovely," Mrs. Harper gushed. "I've searched high and low for a suitable replacement but couldn't find anything close to your spectacular chocolate torte."

"I appreciate the endorsement. Let me make sure I've got everything you asked for." Maya finalized the menu details and date. "I can deliver your order two hours before the party. Will that work?"

"That's perfect, dear. I'm sorry your vacation plans were canceled."

"So am I," she murmured. "Thank you, again, and

I'll call you a few days before to confirm your order." She ended the call and dropped her head in her hands.

December had always been Maya's favorite month and she typically had her shop, Maya's Sweet Spot, decorated for Christmas the weekend following Thanksgiving. This year, instead of pulling out her decorations and shopping for more as soon as the calendar changed to November, she would be spending the time returning the few remaining wedding gifts from people who obviously missed the memo that her Christmas wedding had been called off.

"Hey, Maya."

Her head came up at the sound of her best friend and business partner Rhonda Davis's voice. With Rhonda's five-ten height, slender curves and a face that could stop traffic, Maya often teased her, saying Rhonda would be better suited as a high-fashion model instead of managing a bakery. "Hey, girl. How was your vacation?"

"It was great to spend time with my family, especially my grandmother, since I haven't seen her in a year. She's going to spend the entire month with my parents and go back home after Thanksgiving." She claimed the chair across from Maya's desk. "How did it go with your family?"

Maya shrugged. "Fine, I guess…if you don't count all the 'poor baby' and 'you'll find someone else' comments."

"That sucks. I'm sorry."

"Why? You weren't the one who decided two months before our wedding that you changed your mind and wanted to take your life in a different direction." Maya's ex-fiancé, Stephen Jacobs, had been a no-show at their engagement party—one that had been postponed twice because of his busy schedule. When she finally caught up with him the next day, his only words were "You should be glad I changed my mind before the wedding." No apology and no offer to pay half of the many cancellation costs. Nothing. She got angry all over again thinking about it.

"Ouch!"

She was instantly contrite. "I'm sorry for snapping at you, Rhonda. It's not your fault Stephen was a jerk. And, before you say anything," Maya said, raising her palms in mock surrender, "I know, I know, you tried to warn me that something wasn't right. Too bad I didn't listen."

Rhonda chuckled. "Next time."

"Please. There isn't going to be a next time."

"Humph. What you need is to indulge in a little holiday cheer with a fine, sexy man to get over Stephen. You know, giving thanks for some good toe-curling sex…a little mistletoe action… Trust me, there's no better way to jump-start the holiday season. It'll work wonders," she added with a smug smile.

Maya groaned. "I don't even want to know. Thanks, but no, thanks. I'll pass."

"Okay, but I'm telling you… Anyway, what happened to the decorations? You usually have everything pulled out by now. Didn't we just flip the calendar to November? I expected to see twenty sales papers on your desk. I even brought my walking shoes because I knew you were going to drag me shopping."

"I'm not really feeling the holiday spirit this year."

Rhonda stood, rounded the desk and pulled Maya out of her chair. "Come on, girl. You can't let that idiot ruin your favorite time of year. When we're done, Maya's Sweet Spot is going to be the best-decorated shop *anywhere*."

She smiled, unable to resist her friend's enthusiasm. "Oh, all right. But now that I'm going to stay open, I have twice the orders to take care of. It's a good thing, too. With the way all these stores are closing, I need to do everything I can to stay above water." Ever since the grocery store on the lot adjacent to her shop closed a year ago, the other businesses in the strip mall had shut down, one at a time, until only a handful of small shops remained, including hers.

"Speaking of that, I just saw the owner of the clothing boutique next door and she told me she received a letter from some real estate developer offering to buy her out. Apparently, they want to rezone this block for residential use."

"*What?* No, no, no. They can't do that."

"Wanna bet?" Rhonda wagged a finger. "See, I told you something was up. There's no way four stores are going to be closing at the same time. And then there was that guy."

"What guy?"

"Remember the guy in the suit I saw snooping around last month?"

"Yeah," Maya answered absently, still trying to wrap her mind around what Rhonda said. She had chosen this LA location because of its high visibility and constant foot traffic from several office buildings and a nearby residential area. After two years, she was finally turning a decent profit and had just paid her parents back the money they had lent her to start her business. Now someone was trying to steal her dream. Rhonda's voice pulled her back into the conversation.

"I knew he was up to no good—taking measurements and snapping pictures. Did you get a letter?"

She frowned. "No. I went through all the mail on my desk this morning and I didn't see anything."

"Maybe it's on my desk." Rhonda crossed the room and sat at the desk facing Maya's. She riffled through a stack of envelopes and held up one. "This may be it. The return address says EJJ Developers."

Maya came to stand behind Rhonda and read the letter. Dread settled in her belly. She didn't care how much money they offered, she wasn't selling.

"What are you going to do?" Rhonda asked.

"Nothing. I'm not selling."

"It says here that he'll meet with you at your convenience to discuss the offer, and there's a phone number."

"Fine. I'll call and tell him not to waste his time."

"You think it's going to be that easy?"

Maya released a deep sigh. "No, but my answer won't change. You know how long we searched for the perfect location. I'm not about to just hand over the keys."

"I hear you, Maya, but this is big business. They make a living running over the little guy."

"Well, they need to prepare for the fight of their lives, because this 'little guy' refuses to be run over." She hadn't gotten this far in her thirty years of life by rolling over and didn't plan to start now.

Rhonda stood and embraced her. "Girl, we've been fighting together a long time. You know I've got your back."

"I know." Maya and Rhonda had been best friends since ninth grade and had been there for each other through thick and thin. "If we're going to decorate, we need to get going. I have a lot to do this week and I have to prepare for Mr. Capshaw's party on Saturday."

"Saturday? He usually has his annual company holiday party the second week of December. Why is he having it a month early?"

"Apparently, he's combining it with some business venture he's celebrating. He's having cocktails, appetizers and desserts." She hesitated. "This year it's at the Bonaventure."

"Are you going to be okay delivering? I can do it for you."

Maya nodded. "I can't avoid going places just because they remind me of Stephen."

"True, but you were planning to have your wedding reception there. Really, I can take care of it. I may not set the table as elegantly as you do, but I promise it'll be nice," Rhonda added wryly.

Maya chuckled. "Thanks. I can handle it." She had to. Her business depended on it.

"Okay, if you're sure. I just thought of something. Doesn't the hotel have their own catering staff?"

"They do, and I asked about that. Mr. Capshaw said he'd taken care of it."

"I guess it pays to have some clout."

"It does and I'm glad. He's one of my best customers. Let's get started. I have a feeling it's going to be a long week."

Three months ago, Maya's world was perfect. Now not only had her heart been broken, but she also stood to lose her business. She could *not* let that happen.

Ian Jeffries sat alone at a corner table in the ballroom nursing a drink. He would rather be spending his Saturday evening at home watching college football, but his father asked if he and his brother, Chris, could represent their family's real estate development company at David Capshaw's holiday party. As the man was one of the investors in their latest development project, Ian couldn't very well say no. He scanned the ballroom again in search of his brother, who, so far, hadn't made an appearance. Ian planned to stay only an hour, but it was now going on two hours and he felt his frustration mounting. Lifting the glass, he took a small sip and set it on the table before pulling out his phone to check the game scores again.

"What's up, little brother?"

Ian set the phone on the table. "About damn time you showed up."

Chris laughed and lowered his body in the chair next to Ian. "It can't be that bad."

He snorted. "I hate these things. You could've just come alone, since you enjoy all this *socializing*."

"If you had spent more time talking to people instead of being holed up in your room drawing when we were growing up, your people skills would be better."

"Ha-ha, funny. My people skills are just fine. And if I hadn't been doing all that drawing, we wouldn't be here now." Ian's architectural skills and keen business sense had helped to move their family company from a small real estate business to a full-service firm—owning their own equipment, taking care of all construction from breaking ground to the final walk-through and having dependable contractors. He had done some of the smaller jobs alone but up to now had worked with one of the more experienced architects on bigger projects. It had taken close to a year to convince his father to let him design this latest project solo—one of the company's largest undertakings to date. This would be his first major project and he had no intention of messing it up, hence the reason he was sitting in this hotel ballroom.

"True, that," Chris said. "I don't know how you do it, but you can get the devil to buy air-conditioning."

"It's those *people skills*," Ian said sarcastically.

"Damn, somebody's in a foul mood. Lighten up. It's the holiday season. You know…being thankful…the season to be jolly."

"I'm not in a foul mood," he grumbled, glancing down at his watch again. "I'd just rather be somewhere else."

"Hot date?"

"No."

"Maybe that's your problem. When was the last time you had a little release? You know how you get when you haven't gotten any in a while."

"None of your business. And I don't know what you're talking about."

"We're in a room full of beautiful women. I'm sure at least one of them wouldn't mind putting you out of your misery."

Ian frowned and tried to remember his last liaison. He mentally counted and realized it had been almost six months. He had been so busy working to get this latest project off the ground that he'd put his social life on hold. And he needed some distance from women. His scowl deepened as he recalled how the woman he thought loved him only wanted to use him. He shook off the memories. Maybe he did need a little female company to take the edge off. He surveyed the room. As his brother pointed out, the ballroom was full of beautiful women, a few of whom were staring his way with sultry smiles. Yet none of them held his attention.

"It is the start of the holiday season—a perfect time to wind down. Or…you can always settle down with one woman. There's nothing better than going home to the love of my life."

"No, thanks. I like a little variety." Marriage wasn't on his radar for the foreseeable future. He was only thirty-two, so what was the big rush? Besides, he had already tried the relationship thing and it had almost ruined his family's company and him in the process. Ian had promised himself that it wouldn't happen again.

"That's only because you haven't found that one special woman."

"Because she doesn't exist," Ian countered. He smiled at a woman staring at him as she moved her body on the dance floor.

"How do you know? You're not looking."

"You're right," he answered, still checking out the women in the room. "Anyway, what took you so long to get here?"

Chris leaned back in his chair and smiled. "My beautiful wife and I have decided to start a family. I'm doing my part to make it happen and…let's just say I lost track of time."

"Congratulations. Shellie is going to make a terrific mom."

"Yes, she is. And because this will be our first Christmas together since we got married, I'm leaving her a little gift every day for the month of December. I'm going to get a kick out of watching her open each one."

"I'm sure she'll love that." Ian continued to scan the room until his gaze landed on a woman standing at a dessert table. Unlike other women in the room who were decked out in gowns and jewels, she wore a simple white long-sleeved blouse and black skirt that caressed the sweet curve of her hips and ended just below the knee, robbing him of a complete view of her shapely legs. Her hair was piled on top of her head in some kind of bun.

"Now, that's one gift I wouldn't mind opening," he murmured. Ian couldn't take his eyes off her. She leaned forward to reach for something, and her skirt pulled tighter across her apple-round bottom. His breath caught and his groin tightened. Yeah, he'd been on lockdown way too long. After several minutes, she hadn't moved. He stared curiously. Was she having that much difficulty choosing a dessert? Another minute passed and he stood. "I'll be back."

"Where are you going?" Chris asked.

"I think I'll check out the desserts."

Chris followed Ian's gaze to the table and chuckled. "The desserts *on* the table or the one standing in *front* of the table? I guess the drought will be over soon." He lifted his glass in a mock toast. "Here's to hoping she'll improve your disposition. Can't have you ruining the holidays, Scrooge."

"Shut up, Chris," Ian said as he walked away. When he got closer to the table, he finally caught a glimpse of her face. The woman had an understated beauty—a girl-next-door kind of look—that piqued his interest. His gaze was drawn to her mouth as she bit on her gloss-slicked lips and he imagined nibbling on their lush fullness.

Ian stood next to her for a full minute, inhaling her intoxicating fragrance, and she never noticed him. "Is it that hard to decide on a dessert?"

She startled slightly and whipped her head in his direction. "I'm sorry. Did you say something?" Her dark eyes mirrored confusion.

He smiled. "I asked if you were having a difficult

time choosing a dessert. You've been standing here for a while." He surveyed the vast assortment covering the table—individually proportioned cheesecakes, tortes, truffles, mousses and more. "Although I can see why you'd be having a hard time. Everything looks exquisite." Ian had had a sweet tooth for as long as he could remember, and chocolate was his favorite…food and women. And the brown-sugar beauty standing next to him topped his favorites list at the moment.

"No. I was just making sure everything was laid out the way I want."

His brow lifted. "You're working? You made these?"

"Yes. What do you think?"

"It looks amazing. What do you suggest?"

"Depends on what you like."

A slow grin spread across his lips. "Chocolate. Rich, decadent, sinful…" His gaze traveled slowly down her body and back up to her face. He leaned close to her ear and whispered, "Chocolate." He heard her sharp intake of breath.

"Um… I…you can try the chocolate raspberry truffle bars, chocolate torte with a ganache, triple chocolate mocha truffles or the black-and-white pudding parfait." She pointed to each one with a trembling finger.

"What's the black-and-white pudding parfait?"

"It's chocolate pudding topped with white-chocolate whipped cream."

"Hmm, I may have to try that one later." He could think of a few ways to eat that pudding and none of them involved using a spoon.

"And there's always the chocolate fountain for dipping."

"Yes, there is." Another image flashed in his mind.

"I think for now I'll take one of these triple chocolate mocha truffles and a dance."

"Dance?"

He nodded slowly and bit into the truffle. "This is amazing."

"I can't dance with you."

"Why not?"

"I'm supposed to be working."

He grasped her hand and gently led her out to the dance floor. "Everything on that table is perfect. I'm sure one dance won't get you into trouble." Ian pulled her into his arms and started moving to the slow tune playing. Feeling her soft curves pressed against his and being engulfed in her scent robbed him of all rational thought. The only thing on his mind was finding out how that chocolate would taste on her skin.

Chapter 2

The moment the sexy stranger wrapped his arms around her, sensations Maya never experienced coursed through her body. Her nerves were already on overload from his verbal play at the table. She tried to pull away, but he tightened his arms around her and held her closer to his hard body. She resisted for a short moment, then brought her arms up around his neck and melted into his embrace.

At length he said, "My apologies. I should have introduced myself first. I'm Ian Jeffries, and you are?"

She lifted her head. "Maya. Maya Brooks."

Staring at her with an intensity that heated her insides, he said, "It's a pleasure to meet you, Maya."

"Nice to meet you, too." Pulling away from his magnetic gaze, she turned her head and closed her eyes. His deep voice, handsome face and seductive smile had turned her knees to jelly and impaired her ability to think and talk. Her inner voice screamed that she should get far away from Ian as fast as she could. A man like him could make a woman sell her soul for just one kiss. And why did he have to smell so good?

It had been a long time since she was in a man's arms, so ignoring that pesky voice, Maya settled more comfortably in his arms as the music continued to play. It was only a dance… Although the calendar said it was the beginning of November, the room had been transformed to a winter wonderland, exactly as she imagined it would have been for her wedding reception. Tonight, she could pretend. The heat of his hand sliding sensually down her back penetrated the cotton blouse as if it were on her bare skin, and she bit back a moan. She had dated Stephen for a year and couldn't remember him ever being able to set her body on fire with just a simple pass of his hand.

Maya lifted her eyes to meet his at the same time he turned his head. Their mouths were so close she could feel the heat of his breath. He leaned forward and she tilted her chin. Suddenly, she remembered they were standing in the middle of a ballroom and she was supposed to be working. She stumbled backward and Ian pulled her flush against his body. An involuntary moan slipped from her lips.

"Careful," Ian said with a chuckle.

"I… I have to get back to work." She stepped out of his arms, made a beeline toward the exit and hastily glanced around the room to see if Mr. Capshaw had noticed. She spotted him standing with a small group of men, laughing heartily, and breathed a sigh of relief. As soon as Maya pushed through the door, a tug on her hand stopped her.

"Maya, wait."

"Ian, I need to get back to my job," she said without turning around.

"How much longer do you have to work?"

Truthfully, there wasn't anything else she needed to do. The hotel staff would take care of replenishing the desserts as needed, but Maya prided herself on offering the best services to her clients and often stayed around for a while to ensure that there were no problems. Tonight, however, she was torn between fleeing the hotel as fast as she could and dancing the night away with the fine man still idly rubbing his thumb in small circles in her palm. "An hour or so," she said breathlessly.

Ian turned her to face him. "Do you have to work tomorrow?"

"No," she answered hesitantly. Her shop was closed on Sundays.

A slow grin made its way across Ian's face. "I'll wait for you." He kissed her and, instead of going back into the ballroom, sauntered off down the hallway.

Maya slumped against the wall and took in several deep breaths to calm her pounding heart. No denying she was attracted to Ian, but after the mess she had gone through with her ex, she shouldn't be entertaining thoughts of even talking to a man. Pushing off the wall, she made her way to the kitchen and made arrangements to pick up her containers.

"Oh, there you are," the executive chef called in his heavily accented English, coming toward her, a wide grin plastered on his face.

Her brow lifted a fraction at the stark change in his demeanor. When she first arrived, he had been curt and none too happy that she had been contracted to provide the desserts instead of his staff. She curbed the urge to glance behind her to see if he was talking to someone else.

"My dear, these desserts are simply divine. I must say my favorite is the black-and-white pudding parfait. It's a chocolate lover's dream! Would you mind if I kept your contact information...for a few special occasions?" he added, lowering his voice to a whisper.

"I left my cards in my car."

"No worries." He rushed over to a table, came back and pushed a small card and pen in her hand.

The mention of chocolate conjured up an image of her and Ian at the dessert table—his nearness, piercing midnight eyes, smooth-as-honey voice—and a rush of heat spread through her body. The man had a way with words. Still thinking about Ian, she absently scribbled her address on the card and handed it back. "Thank you so much for your kind words. It means a lot coming from you."

"No, thank *you*, Maya. Are you sure I can't lure you away to come work for me?"

Maya chuckled. "I'm flattered, but I enjoy working for myself."

He shrugged. "Can't blame a guy for trying."

"Is there anything else you need me to take care of?"

"No. My staff will take care of everything."

"I'll drop by on Monday morning to pick up my containers." They engaged in polite conversation for a few minutes, and then Maya left. The chef's staff had everything under control and this would be the perfect time to slip out before Ian noticed she was gone. Something about the way he held and kissed her told her this man was dangerous to her psyche and she didn't want to risk another encounter with him. But the perfectionist in Maya wouldn't let her leave without checking the table one last time.

* * *

Ian walked directly to the hotel's registration desk. Holding Maya in his arms had set off a raging desire within him that only she could satisfy. He didn't know how he would accomplish it, but he had to convince her to spend the night with him.

"May I help you, sir?" the smiling clerk asked.

"Yes. I'd like to book a room for the night."

She clicked a few keys on her computer. "There are no standard rooms available, but I do have a one-bedroom suite. It has a living area with a sleeper sofa, wet bar—"

He removed a credit card from his wallet and placed it on the counter. "Even better." He planned for them to use every square inch of that suite. Ian signed the paper, put the card back into his wallet and accepted the room key.

"Enjoy your stay, Mr. Jeffries."

"I plan to. Thank you." He stopped at the gift shop first and then went up to his room to deposit the bag. Ian took a quick peek at his watch. He had forty minutes to come up with a way to persuade Maya to go along with his proposal. As soon as he entered the ballroom, Mr. Capshaw called out to him.

"Ian, there you are."

"How are you, Mr. Capshaw? Nice party."

He laughed heartily. "I can't think of a better way to start the holiday season, and we have a lot to celebrate this year." Capshaw's slightly slurred voice indicated that the man had probably reached his limit two drinks ago.

"Yes, we do," Ian agreed.

"Grab your brother and meet me at my table where the other investors are sitting."

Ian walked back to where Chris sat talking on the phone. He tapped Chris on the shoulder.

"Okay, I'll be home soon," Chris was saying. He hung up and glanced up at Ian with a grin. "Where's the woman you were dancing with? You must be losing your touch."

"I haven't lost anything. She's working."

"Working?"

"Yeah. She made the desserts. Man, you have to try the triple-chocolate mocha truffles."

"She works for the hotel?"

He shrugged. "I assume so. Mr. Capshaw wants us to meet him over at the table with the investors."

"Good. We can talk to them for a few minutes, and then be out of here."

"Actually, I'm going to stay awhile longer."

"I thought you were anxious to leave," Chris said, rising to his feet. "Your change in plans wouldn't have anything to do with the woman who just entered, would they?"

"Maybe." Ian followed his brother's gaze and saw Maya heading toward the dessert table with another hotel employee. Their eyes locked for a brief moment before she turned away to focus on whatever the other woman was saying. A bump on his shoulder drew him out of his thoughts.

"Mr. Capshaw is waiting," Chris reminded Ian.

Giving Maya one last look, Ian followed his brother over to where the investors had gathered on the other side of the room. After a round of handshakes, Mr. Capshaw proposed a toast to the partnership.

One of the men asked, "Are we on schedule for the groundbreaking?"

Chris cut a quick look at Ian before answering. "We've run into a small hiccup, but—"

"What kind of hiccup?" Mr. Capshaw asked.

"One of the business owners doesn't want to sell. Someone from our office plans to meet with the owner this week, and I'm sure contract negotiations will follow."

"That's good to hear," Mr. Capshaw said, raising his glass.

Ian and Chris excused themselves minutes later. Once in the hallway, Ian said, "I thought all the owners accepted the offers."

Chris scrubbed a hand across his forehead. "I thought so, too. But Sam told me yesterday that there's one owner who called and said she had no intentions of selling."

"Great. This is my first major project since that mess a year ago. It took forever to convince Dad to give me another shot, and I don't need this."

"It's not the same, Ian. No one is deliberately trying to sabotage you."

"The result will be the same. Now what?"

"Sam is going to talk to the owner this week, increase the offer and hope she'll come around. I can't see her turning down an amount significantly over what the building is worth."

"Let's hope not. That would ruin my holiday for sure."

"Two years in a row...oh, hell no! You were such a grouch last year you could give Scrooge a run for his money. If Sam can't make any headway with her, we might need you to step away from your drafting table and work your magic."

"I'll do whatever it takes. Keep me posted." Ian

checked the time again. "I'm going back in. I don't want to miss Maya."

"Maya?" Chris asked with a laugh. "I guess it didn't take long for her to get your attention, which is odd."

"Why?"

"You never react to women this way, especially when it's someone you're only looking to have a one-night stand with. Which makes me wonder about this particular woman."

Ian frowned. "I don't follow."

"I always told you that when the love bug bit you, you were going to go down *hard*. Looks like it's your turn, little brother. See you around."

Ian muttered a curse, telling Chris exactly what he could do with that statement, pivoted on his heel and walked away.

Chris's laughter echoed through the hall behind Ian.

He pushed through the ballroom doors, immediately sought out Maya and spotted her at the far end near the other exit. He strode purposely across the room, ignoring two women who tried to detain him. "Maya," he called when he was in earshot.

She turned, seemingly surprised to see him. "Ian. I thought you'd left."

His brow lifted. "Why? I told you I'd wait. Are you off work yet?"

"I…" She nodded.

"Good." Ian led her to the dance floor and gathered her in his arms. "I want to dance with you again." He held her close and swayed to the ballad the band played, loving the way she fit in his arms. "Maya."

"Hmm."

"Are you in a rush to leave?"

"Well…um, no."

"Would you join me for a drink? Just to talk."

"Okay."

He smiled, took her hand and led her out off the dance floor. He stopped to grab another truffle first, then led her out to the bar. It took a moment, but he spotted a table at the far side and hurried over before someone else could claim it. The waitress came to take their order.

"A glass of Chardonnay, please," Maya said.

"I'll have a cognac." Ian never drank his first one. After the woman left, he focused on Maya. "So, are you some kind of chef?"

Maya smiled. "I'm a pastry chef."

"How long have you been a pastry chef?"

"Professionally, six years. But I've been fascinated with baking and chocolate for as long as I can remember."

"If everything else tastes as good as that truffle, I'd say you've perfected the art. I'm looking forward to sampling a few more of your delicious treats," he said. The waitress came back with their drinks. "Thanks." Ian lifted his glass. "To great conversation."

She touched her glass to his and took a sip of her wine.

"I've never met a pastry chef. Seems like it would be hard work to come up with all those different desserts."

"Not really. Many of them are well-known recipes and others are those that I've tweaked to make them my own. What about you?"

"I like to draw, so I became an architect."

"That has to be fascinating."

He chuckled. "It has its moments."

"Did you grow up in LA?"

"Born and bred."

They both laughed. They spent the remainder of the evening swapping childhood stories.

Maya glanced down at her watch. "Wow. I didn't realize it was so late."

Ian took a peek at his. Over two hours had passed. "Neither did I." He paid the bill, then escorted her out to the lobby.

"Thank you for the drink, Ian. I had a great time."

"So did I. I'm not ready for it to end."

"Neither am I," she said softly.

"Spend the night with me, Maya."

Her gaze flew to his. "What?"

He stared intently into her eyes and repeated the question. "Just one night to explore whatever it is that's happening between us."

Maya shook her head. "Ian, I don't... I can't...we don't even know each other."

"We will by morning," he said, capturing her mouth in an urgent kiss. Ian lifted his head. "One night," he implored. His eyes were riveted to the rapid beating of the pulse in her neck and he knew she was just as affected. "Tell me you don't feel this attraction, and I'll walk away now."

"You know I do." She stared up at him for several charged seconds, then nodded.

Ian released the breath he had been holding. "I promise you won't be disappointed."

Maya shook her head again. "No promises, Ian. I don't want anything beyond tonight."

"Then we're in agreement. The only promise I'll make is a night of pleasure you won't ever forget." He lowered his head and nibbled on her lush bottom lip. When her lips parted, he slid his tongue inside and kissed her slowly, provocatively, giving her a taste of what he planned to do to her. Her body trembled and she moaned. Ian was as hard as a steel beam and he needed to get her upstairs now.

Chris's words rushed back to Ian. *I always told you that when the love bug bit you, you were going to go down hard.* She definitely fascinated Ian, but he'd only known Maya for a few hours, so it wasn't love. However, one thing about Chris's statement was true—Ian had never reacted so strongly toward a woman.

Chapter 3

What are you doing agreeing to a one-night stand? Maya's inner voice screamed. Too bad she didn't have an answer. She had never done something so bold in all her life. Her mind and body were at odds but, somehow, clearly her body had gained the upper hand. She felt like she was in one of those old cartoons with the angel on one shoulder and the devil on the other. The sensible side of her said women did not sleep with a man they just met, that she should date for a while and then see. But there was a side of Maya begging to get out that argued, *Sensible and practical is overrated. Isn't that what you did with Stephen? And look where that got you?* This was so unlike her. She hadn't even asked where they were going. For all she knew, he could be a serial killer. Okay, she didn't believe that last part, but still. She glanced around the hotel lobby. At least there would be dozens of witnesses. Then again, last-minute reservations were expensive.

"Maya?"

She blinked and realized Ian was talking. "I'm sorry. What did you say?"

"I said I hope you don't mind that I reserved a room here."

"No. Wait. When did you reserve a room?" Maya's first thought was relief, then curiosity.

Ian grinned sheepishly. "Right after I left you earlier. Are you having second thoughts?"

"Um…no." Actually, she was flattered. Stephen had never taken the initiative to even make dinner reservations.

He squeezed her hand and smiled. "I'm glad. Can you excuse me? I need to speak to the concierge for a minute."

"Okay." She watched him confidently stroll across the lobby. The man certainly knew how to command a room. She put him close to six feet tall—wearing a pale gray suit she knew had never touched the rack—clean shaven, closed-cropped black hair, smooth coffee-with-cream skin and eyes. Several women did double takes as he passed. In fact, one woman stopped, turned and stared with her mouth hanging open. Maya chuckled.

"Ready?" Ian asked when he returned.

She took his extended hand and walked with him to the elevators. The reflective glass elevators rose swiftly, making the city lights pass by in a blur. Maya continued to have mixed emotions about what she was getting ready to do while they rode the elevator up to their floor. As much as she tried to deny it, Stephen's deception had been a major blow to her self-esteem and some part of her wanted…no, needed to feel desirable again. And Ian made her feel that way. Tonight, she decided, would be all about her. Tomorrow she could go back to her old, practical self. The elevator came to a halt on the thirtieth floor and she allowed him to guide her down the hall. He stopped at a door, unlocked it and stepped back to let her enter. Her gaze swept over the room and she realized he had booked a suite. Maya jumped slightly when Ian came up behind her and placed his hands on her shoulders. He turned her to face him and she tried to hide her embarrassment.

"Nervous?" Ian asked.

She nodded. "A little." That wasn't exactly the truth. She was *a lot* nervous.

Ian angled his head and stared intently at her. He obviously sensed it, because he pulled her into his embrace and said, "Maya, I want you, but if you're having second thoughts we don't have to do anything."

She knew he wanted her, felt the solid ridge of his erection pressed against her belly and read the desire in his eyes. She also saw honesty reflected in his face and it had a calming effect on her nerves. "I want you, too."

"Good. I want to kiss you again."

"That's all?"

He chuckled low and dark. "Sweetheart, kissing you is just the start of what I want to do to you…what I'm *going* to do to you." Ian lifted her hand and placed a lingering kiss on the back, turned her palm up and circled his tongue over the pulse point on her wrist.

Her breath hitched. Electricity shot from her arm straight to her core and she felt a rush of moisture between her thighs.

"I hope you don't have anywhere to be tomorrow," he murmured, still teasing the pulse point. "I plan to touch, taste and explore every delectable inch of your gorgeous body. When I'm done, neither of us will be able to move."

Maya's eyes widened when his statement filtered through her haze of desire. What had she gotten herself into? Before she formed a reply to his heated promise, he slanted his mouth over hers in a kiss that was hot, hard and literally made her weak. He tasted of chocolate and cognac. The heady combination sent her senses spiraling out of control and she gripped the lapels of his suit coat to keep from sliding to the floor. Desire unlike anything she had ever felt raced through her body and she trembled as his tongue made sweeping, swirling motions inside her mouth. He brought his hands up to frame her face, holding her in place and delving deeper. When he finally lifted his head, Maya was breathing like she had run a marathon.

"Mmm," Ian said.

"What are you doing to me?" she asked, still trying to catch her breath.

A wicked gleam leaped into his eyes. "Tasting you."

Oh. My. God!

He leaned forward again, but was interrupted by a knock on the door. "Ah, right on time." He stepped around her and went to open the door.

She tilted her head, puzzled. A hotel employee entered pushing a cart with two covered domes. Ian tipped the man and closed the door behind him. "Did you order dinner?"

A smile played around the corners of Ian's mouth and he shook his head. "It's a little dessert." He lifted the covers to reveal a bowl of strawberries, a bowl of melted chocolate and two servings of the black-and-white pudding parfait.

Maya laughed. "Is that from Mr. Capshaw's party?"

"I told you chocolate is my favorite."

"Well, go ahead." He shrugged out of his jacket, loosened and removed the tie and then tossed them on the sofa. Next, he went to work on his shirt. Keeping his eyes trained on her, he undid the buttons, one by one, until it hung open. Her mouth ran dry when he discarded it, leaving him in trousers that hung low on a trim waist. Lean muscular arms, defined chest with a light dusting of hair and washboard abs. *Chiseled chocolate!* She was so busy gawking she didn't realize he had moved until he stood in front of her, and had undone the first button on her blouse.

"Will you trust me tonight, Maya?" Ian asked, his fingers lightly tracing the tops of her breasts above her bra.

There was something about the way this man touched her. "Trust you?"

"Yes. Will you trust me to give you pleasure? If you don't like something, you can stop me at any time." He bent and replaced his fingers with his tongue.

Maya could hardly talk. "Ye…yes." For one night it would be about her and she wanted everything he had to give.

He continued unbuttoning her blouse. "Nice. Sexy."

She glanced down at her black lace-edged bra. Thank goodness she'd had the presence of mind to wear matching underwear.

He helped her out of the top and carefully laid it across the corner of the chair, then reached behind her to lower the zipper on her skirt. Ian squatted down. "Step out."

She did as he asked, along with the sensible two-inch pumps she always wore when working.

"I've been wanting to touch these beautiful legs all night," he said, skimming his hands along her calves, up her thighs, and dragging her panties down and off. He came to his feet.

Maya started shaking again. "I... I thought you were going to have dessert."

Ian picked up one of the parfaits, snaked an arm around her waist and walked her backward to the large table. "I am." He dipped his finger in the whipped cream, smeared it across her lips and proceeded to lick it off. He groaned. "Absolutely delicious." He dug out another portion, this time a mixture of the cream and the pudding, and made a path from her neck to the top of her breasts.

The sensation of the cool dessert followed by the scorching heat of his tongue sent shivers down her spine, and all she could do was brace herself against the table and moan. "Ian," she whispered.

"Do you like that?"

"Yes."

"What about this?" Ian unclasped and removed her bra. He smeared the pudding across her breasts, then made sweeping circles around her breast until he reached her nipple. He took the hardened bud into his mouth and sucked, repeating the action with the other breast. "You taste so good, so sweet."

Her eyes slid closed and Maya managed a strangled moan. She couldn't even begin to respond to his question. Never had a man done to her the things Ian was doing now, or made her feel so alive.

"I take that as a yes. Well, let's see how you like this."

She felt a warm sensation and looked down to see him drizzling the warm melted chocolate in a path from her chest to her belly and disappearing between her legs. He picked up a hulled strawberry, dipped it in the chocolate pooled in her belly button and, holding her gaze, brought it to his lips. The sight turned her on even more.

"Mmm. The strawberry is good, the chocolate better, but neither compares to the delectable flavor of your skin." He picked up another berry, dipped it and smeared the chocolate across her lips.

Maya snaked her tongue out and licked the chocolate from his finger, then drew the strawberry into her mouth, chewing slowly. Emboldened by his play, she took some of the chocolate, rubbed it across the muscular planes of his chest and licked it clean. "Mmm, yes. It's *very* good." She smiled, delighting in his sharp intake of breath and the tremor in his body from her touch.

Ian lifted her and laid her down on the table. "You missed a spot," he said, sucking gently on her bottom lip.

The table was cold beneath Maya's back, a stark contrast to Ian's hot mouth and hands. He left her mouth, trailed his hands down the front of her body and followed with his mouth. She gasped when she felt the warm liquid on her left inner thigh, then her right one, moving higher and coming close to her already wet center. She writhed and moaned at the exquisite sensation, and her thighs quivered in anticipation. Her hips shot up off the table when he settled between her spread legs, his tongue sweeping across her core in one long stroke.

He groaned. "Damn, baby. Every inch of this sexy body is pure sweetness."

Ian slid one finger inside her, then another, playing her like a finely tuned instrument, while his tongue tapped out its own seductive beat against her clit. The twin assaults were so erotic she didn't last a minute. Maya screamed his name, exploding into a thousand pieces as an orgasm tore through her. She shuddered uncontrollably, her breaths coming in short gasps.

"We're only getting started. There's much more and it gets better," Ian said, rising to his feet. He brought his fingers to his mouth and sucked them clean. "Pure sweetness."

Although she was spent, the carnal sight sent Maya's passions rising again. And how much better could it get? she wondered, still trying to catch her breath.

The rapturous expression on Maya's face combined with the sensual picture she made lying on the table almost made Ian come right then and there. He quickly shed his pants and briefs and searched his pockets for the condoms he had bought. He tore one off, sheathed himself and came back to where she still lay on the table. He pulled her to a sitting position, needing to kiss her again. Without breaking the seal of their mouths, Ian shifted their bodies, stood between her legs and pulled her hips to the edge of the table. He guided himself slowly, inch by incredible inch, inside her. They both groaned. He pulled back and thrust again in a fine, circling motion, loving the way her tight walls clutched him.

Ian lowered Maya back to the table and lifted her legs onto his shoulders, wanting and needing to go deeper. Her passionate cries aroused him further and he increased the pace. He grasped her ankles, spread her thighs wider and thrust harder into her, her breasts moving in tandem. Their breathing grew ragged and sweat broke out on his body as she arched up to meet him stroke for stroke. It felt so good being inside her. He could feel his orgasm building and knew he wouldn't last much longer. Ian drove into her until she cried out wildly, her inner walls contracting around him. Pleasure ripped through him with an intensity that almost blew his head off and he yelled her name. Maya's muscles clenched his throbbing shaft as his body continued to shudder violently. He gently lowered her legs, withdrew and braced his trembling arms on the table.

Several moments later, when he could finally move, Ian swept her into his arms and carried her to the bathroom. They were both sticky from all the chocolate. He started the water and adjusted the temperature. "Go ahead."

"Thanks." She stepped into the shower stall and closed the door behind her.

The water cascading down her body sent heat flowing to his groin and Ian left before he was tempted to join her. But he lost the battle two minutes later and came back. She startled slightly when he came up behind her. "I couldn't stay away," he murmured close to her ear, and stepped into the spray.

Maya turned, circled her arms around his neck, smiled and came up on tiptoes to kiss him. "I'm glad."

That was all it took to snap his control. Ian backed her against the tile wall and pinned her arms above her head as he kissed and caressed his way down her body.

"Ian," she moaned.

"I'm right here." He stepped out of the shower just long enough to don the condom he had wisely placed on the sink. After he turned Maya around, he placed her hands on the wall and then ran his hands down her back and over her hips. He tilted her forward and entered her from behind. She was so tight, so hot. Too far gone, Ian tightened his grip on her waist and set a strong, driving rhythm that made the shower door vibrate. Their moans and cries bounced off the walls as he pounded in and out of her.

"Ian!" Maya convulsed with a loud wail.

Moments later he threw his head back and exploded in a rush of pleasure that forced a raw expletive from his throat and nearly dropped him to his knees. His head fell forward limply. Ian trailed his fingers down her slick spine, then turned her to face him. He stroked a finger down her cheek and placed a soft kiss on her lips. Their eyes locked and he felt a jolt in his midsection. But he pushed it aside, reminding himself that this was just for one night.

Chapter 4

Maya woke up the next morning alone in bed. Glancing over at the clock on the nightstand, she noted it was after ten. She couldn't remember the last time she'd slept past eight, but then again she had not gotten much sleep last night. She listened for sounds of water running in the bathroom but heard nothing. She frowned, strained her ears, listening for movement elsewhere in the suite. Again nothing. Had Ian already left? A wave of disappointment washed over her. Sure, they had agreed on the one night, but she would never have thought he'd leave without so much as a goodbye. However, it was probably a good thing. It would save them both that awkward morning-after moment.

Dragging herself to a sitting position, she groaned softly. Every inch of her body was sore. She padded across the floor to the bathroom to wash her face and brush her teeth with one of the travel kits the hotel had provided. Maya stared at her reflection in the mirror—hair was a tangled mess, lips still kiss swollen and body covered with marks from their passionate encounters. She felt her cheeks warm with the recollection of what had occurred between her and Ian. The man possessed an unbelievable amount of stamina. After the second time in the shower, they slept for a few hours before he woke her in the wee hours of the morning for a third round. She'd had more pleasure in one night with Ian than in one year with Stephen.

Uncomfortable walking around naked, she wrapped herself in a towel and went in search of her clothes. "Ian," she gasped. "You scared me. I thought you left." He was sitting on the edge of the bed when she came out of the bathroom.

"I would never leave without saying goodbye, especially since I'm not ready to say goodbye." Ian rose to his feet and came toward her. He slid his arms around her waist at the same time his head descended, capturing her mouth in a slow, drugging kiss. "Good morning."

Maya's head was still spinning from the kiss and it took a moment for his words to register. "What are you talking about?"

He led her over to the bed and sat next to her. Taking her hand, he said, "Maya, I know we agreed to one night, but I'd like to amend our agreement."

As much as she wanted to see him again, she wasn't sure it would be a good idea. On the other hand… "What kind of amendment?"

"I want to propose that we continue to see each other."

"For how long?"

He shrugged. "For as long as we enjoy each other's company."

She contemplated his offer. An affair with no definitive end could prove to be dangerous. Hell, an affair of any length with this man would be dangerous. She could see herself easily falling for him and didn't want to risk her heart again. But the woman he had unleashed last night wanted more. "Maybe we can see each other until the holidays are over." Hopefully, being with Ian would help ease the sting of her failed engagement.

"What if we still want to see each other when the holidays are over?"

"We won't."

His brow lifted slightly. "What if we do? How about we agree to an affair through the holidays and then reassess our options?"

Certain she would be able to walk away after Christmas, Maya nodded. That would be roughly two months—not enough time to get emotionally attached. "Okay."

"Great! I say we celebrate with breakfast after we shower."

She recalled what had happened the last time they showered together. She was positive the guests in rooms on either side had heard them last night. "Um...you can go first."

He chuckled. "Lucky for you I don't have any more condoms. Otherwise I think I might have to persuade you to take another shower with me."

He rimmed her lips with his tongue and thrust inside when she parted them, forcing her to remember what they had shared. Yeah, it was a good thing he didn't have more. She needed some recovery time.

"More of that chocolate wouldn't be a bad idea, either. Chocolate…your kisses… I can't think of a better combination." Ian kissed her once more and stood. "I'll be out in a few minutes."

She stared at his slender, muscular frame and tight round butt in nothing but those gray boxer briefs and sighed. The man looked scrumptious coming *and* going, and she was sorely tempted to go downstairs for more condoms. That was when she knew she had a problem. The longer she sat, the more she began to rethink extending their affair until she was in a full-blown panic. She wanted him too much, and something told her it wouldn't be easy to walk away from Ian. She couldn't take a chance with her heart again.

Maya hurried through the suite, threw on her clothes and tried to do something with her hair. She had to get out before he finished showering. Dressed, she surveyed the suite for anything she might have missed. Satisfied, she glanced in the direction of the bedroom when she heard the water shut off. She felt bad about the way she was leaving but knew if he touched her, she would never be able to resist. She tipped over, opened the door and closed it quietly behind her. She touched her palm to the door and whispered, "I'm sorry."

Maya hurried down the hall to the elevator and didn't relax until she was in her car and pulling out of the lot. As soon as she got home to her two-bedroom condo, she collapsed on her bed. Sadness engulfed her and she tried to convince herself that she had made the right decision. She dug out her cell phone and turned it on. It immediately chimed, indicating missed messages. Rhonda had sent two texts and called three times between last night and this morning, each message more frantic than the previous one. Before she could listen to the last message, her house phone rang. In an age when most people used their cell phones for everything, Maya's mother insisted that she keep a landline. *You never know when the power will go out. That cell phone won't do nothing for you if you can't charge it,* she always said.

"Girl, where have you been?" Rhonda said as soon as Maya answered. "I've been trying to call you since last night. Are you trying to give me a heart attack? I even called the hotel last night looking for you. I didn't know whether you were safe or lying somewhere in a hospital."

Maya rolled her eyes. "Rhonda, are you finished?"

"I guess. You could've let somebody know you were safe," she muttered. "Are you okay?"

"Yeah. Fine."

"Where were you?"

She was somewhat embarrassed by the fact that she had engaged in a sex-a-thon with a man she had just met and wasn't sure she wanted to share those details.

"Maya, did something happen?"

Sighing heavily, she said, "Yeah. A whole lot happened."

"That doesn't sound good. Did you have a problem with the hotel or Mr. Capshaw? Or did you have a hard time being at the hotel?" she added sympathetically.

"No. That wasn't it. I… I…"

"You what?" Rhonda asked when Maya trailed off.

"I met a man at Mr. Capshaw's party and spent the night at the hotel with him," Maya finally blurted.

There was silence for a full five seconds before Rhonda screamed into the phone. "*Oh, my God!* I don't believe it. You did *what*?"

"I'm not repeating it. You're the one who suggested it. Happy now?"

She giggled. "Are you?"

"It was the most erotic night of my life," she confessed.

Rhonda screamed again. "I'll be over in thirty minutes to hear the details."

Maya heard a loud click and shook her head. She really wanted a long soak in the tub but opted for a shower instead, knowing her friend would be ringing the doorbell in exactly thirty minutes or less. She was just putting her hair into a ponytail when she heard the door. Her hair had gotten wet last night and Maya would have to wash it and flatiron it sometime today.

"Hey, girl," she said, opening the door to Rhonda.

"Hey." She handed Maya a cup and followed her to the living room. "I stopped and got you a decaf mocha. Although, by the looks of you, you could use a shot or two of caffeine," she added slyly. Taking a seat on the sofa, she said, "Okay, spill it. And don't leave anything out."

"Can't I get a chance to enjoy my coffee first?" Maya chuckled at the death glare Rhonda shot her. She dropped down on the sofa and told her how Ian had come over to the dessert table, his verbal play and the dance. "The way he held me… Stephen never made me feel like that the entire year we dated."

Rhonda snorted. "Don't get me started on that jerk. Anyway, how did you get from the dance floor to the bedroom?"

"He came right out and asked me to spend the night. I knew we were attracted to each other, but I never expected him to be so bold."

"Well, don't leave me in suspense." She leaned forward. "How was it?"

"It was all that and *more*!" They both screamed and

giggled like teenagers. "Girl, he had servings of the black-and-white parfait, a bowl of the melted chocolate from the fountain and strawberries sent up to the room and..."

Rhonda screamed again. "What does he look like?"

"His name is Ian and he's about six feet, fine as all get-out, slender muscular build, rich milk-chocolate skin—chiseled chocolate."

Rhonda fanned herself and fell back against the sofa. "Whew. I'm getting warm just hearing about it. Sounds like a night to remember."

Maya smiled. "It was."

"So, are you going to see him again?"

She dropped her head. "It was only supposed to be one night, but he wants us to continue seeing each other. I agreed, but I just got out of one bad relationship. Stephen broke my heart and I don't want to feel that pain again. Ian is charming and I can see myself falling for him. I can't let that happen."

"What are you going to do?"

"I've already done it. I sort of sneaked out while he was in the shower and he doesn't have my phone number," Maya said sheepishly.

Rhonda threw up her hands. "What am I going to do with you? You didn't even give the man a chance."

Maya dropped her head in her hands and groaned. "I know, I know. I feel so bad, especially since I agreed to amend our one-night stand."

"Well, at least you can say you've had your toes curled once in your life."

That she could. But already she was beginning to have regrets about tipping out on Ian. After Rhonda left, Maya spent time going over her schedule, washing her hair and finally having that long soak in the tub.

She was at the shop bright and early Monday morning getting her baked goods ready for the day. She didn't usually have a lot left over, but whatever she had was donated to a local shelter. Halfway through the morning, she left Rhonda to man the store while she went to pick up her containers from the hotel.

The moment she stepped into the Bonaventure Hotel lobby, memories of her night with Ian rose swiftly in her mind. She tried to push them aside to no avail. Wanting to get in and out as soon as possible, Maya quickened her steps. On her way out, she was still chuckling at the chef's pitiful expression at her refusal to work for him. But he did agree to pass her name along to a few people who might want desserts for an intimate gathering and tried to coerce her into giving him the recipe for her black-and-white parfait. The mention of the dessert brought on more heated memories. Her nipples puckered beneath her blouse, and the space between her legs throbbed with the same rhythm Ian had started Saturday night. What she wouldn't give for just one more night.

Wednesday afternoon, Ian sat hunched over his drafting table staring at a blank page. He was supposed to be working on a design for a new senior living complex, but his concentration was at an all-time low. It had been three days since Maya sneaked out of the hotel room, and he couldn't stop thinking about her. When he had emerged from the shower and found her gone, he was angry and more than a little disappointed. Why had she left? He thought they were on the same page, but apparently she'd had second thoughts. Usually, he had no problems moving on from a woman, but Maya wasn't like other women. Something about her had piqued more than a passing interest, and he didn't want to stop and analyze the reasons why. He should probably just let it go and move on. But he couldn't.

An hour later, he gave up all pretense of working. Ian stood, stretched and walked out to his secretary's desk. "Ms. Smith, I'm going to be out of the office for a couple of hours. If something comes up, you can reach me on my cell."

"No problem, Mr. Jeffries."

He was going to the Bonaventure to find Maya. In his car, he cranked up the air-conditioning. Winter was a month away, yet the temperatures still hovered near eighty. On the drive, he thought about what he would say to her. Other than asking why she left, he didn't have a clue. He did know that he was going to have a hard time not dragging her up to a room and continuing what they had started on Saturday. And if he got his hands on some more of that chocolate, all bets were off. For the past three nights, he'd had visions of all the things they had done with those desserts and woke up with a hard-on each morning. That last go-around they had changed positions at least three times and ended up half off the bed. Ian always enjoyed being adventurous in the bedroom, but no other woman had inspired him to use food during foreplay. And he suspected no other woman would. The memory of their kisses came back to him. As much as he enjoyed those truffles, they didn't compare with the sweet taste of her mouth.

Ian parked in the registration area and entered the lobby. "Excuse me, I'm looking for Maya Brooks. She's a pastry chef," he said to the concierge.

The woman frowned. "I don't think we have an employee by that name, but maybe she's new. I'll call the executive chef. He'll be able to help you."

"Thanks." He could have sworn she said she worked at the hotel.

"If you'll follow me, sir."

He followed her to the entrance of an expensive steak house located on the thirty-fifth floor, where a man wearing a chef's jacket waited.

He introduced himself. "Hello. I understand you're looking for one of my employees."

"Yes," Ian said. "Maya Brooks. She provided the desserts for a party here on Saturday night."

"I'm sorry. Maya doesn't work for the hotel. She was contracted directly by the client."

Ian did his best to hide his shock and, yes, panic.

The man folded his arms across his chest and frowned slightly. "Why are you looking for her?"

"I attended the party Saturday and enjoyed several of the desserts." *Enjoyed* probably wasn't the most accurate word, but it was appropriate for the conversation. "I'm planning a small gathering and wanted to see if Ms. Brooks was available," he lied.

"Hmm. What was your favorite?"

"The black-and-white pudding parfait."

The chef's features relaxed. "Mine, too. Isn't it exquisite?"

"It was absolutely unforgettable." *In more ways than one.*

"Well, she did ask me to pass on her information to prospective clients. Wait here and I'll get it."

"Thank you." Ian breathed a sigh of relief. He was one step closer to finding Maya. The chef returned moments later and handed Ian a piece of paper. Ian thanked the man again and hurried off with a huge grin on his face. Back in his car, he programmed the address into his GPS and was surprised to find it was in a residential area. Did she work out of her home? He drummed his fingers on the steering wheel, debating whether to go directly to her house or wait until tonight. Now. He couldn't wait. It was already after four and that made it close to evening, he reasoned. Besides, after getting through the downtown traffic, it would be evening when he arrived. He called his secretary to tell her he would not be returning and then, starting the engine, eased out of the lot and onto the road.

It took him over an hour to get to Maya's place and, luckily, someone was exiting the gate as he reached the entry to her condominium complex. He parked in an uncovered spot, circled back to her unit and rang the bell, hoping she was home. His head came up when the door opened.

"Ian! What are you… How did you… What are you doing here?" Maya asked, surprise clearly evident in her voice.

He drank in the sight of her and let his gaze wander over her luscious body in a fitted T-shirt and skimpy shorts, and standing barefoot. Every detail of their night together came rushing back, and his body reacted in kind. She wasn't out of his system. Not by a long shot.

Chapter 5

Maya couldn't believe Ian was standing at her door.
How had he gotten her address?

"You left without saying goodbye."

"I—"

Ian moved closer until their bodies were touching.
"Invite me in, Maya," he whispered against her lips.
When she nodded, he backed her into the house and
shut the door behind him, pulling her into his arms and
slanting his mouth over hers.

Heat shot to her core and she moaned in his mouth.
Their tongues tangled and danced and she felt herself
losing control. Maya broke off the kiss.

He eased back and rested his forehead against hers.
"Why did you leave?"

"How did you get my address?"

He smiled. "The chef. He said you told him to pass
along your information to interested clients," Ian clarified.

She remembered being distracted and thinking about Ian. Had she written down her home address instead of the one to her shop?

"You didn't answer my question."

Maya exhaled deeply. "I don't know. I just started thinking and…" She turned and walked over to the sofa and sat.

He followed, lowered himself next to her and took her hand. "Talk to me, Maya. I thought we were in agreement. Did I do something, say something?"

"No, no. It's nothing like that."

"Then what is it?"

She closed her eyes briefly to gather her thoughts. "Ian, two months ago I was engaged and had planned to get married next month."

He tried to hide his shock.

"That all changed when my ex decided he wanted to take his life in a different direction, namely one with a woman whose father could give him better access to the corporate ladder he was determined to climb," she added wryly. "I know I agreed to something casual, but I really don't know if I can do that right now."

Ian's jaw tightened. "I'm sorry, Maya. I don't know what to say."

"I'm sorry, too."

"I still want to see you."

"I want to see you, too, but…"

"I can't even imagine how much he hurt you, but you're a beautiful woman, too beautiful to lock yourself away. Can we just keep with our agreement and see where it goes?"

She needed to stop looking into those eyes that threatened to suck her in. And he *really* needed to stop touching her. There was no way she could stick to her decision with his hands on her. "Ian, I…ohhh." Now he was playing dirty, bringing his lips into the action. He wrapped an arm around her shoulder and trailed kisses along the curve of her jaw and neck.

"We'll have so much fun together," he said, still kissing his way to her chest.

Maya's eyes slid closed and she breathed a sigh of surrender. She reached up, brought Ian's face to hers, and gave him a slow and sultry kiss.

"What are you doing tonight?" Ian asked when they came up for air.

"I don't have anything planned. Why?"

"I'd like to take you out to dinner. And before you say no, you skipped out on brunch, so you kind of owe me," he added with a sly grin.

A surge of guilt rose and Maya felt her face flush. "I know. I feel really bad about that."

Ian did his best to look sad, but the smile playing around the corners of his mouth ruined it. "Left me all alone and starving."

She burst out laughing. "Yeah, right. You look like you haven't eaten in days."

His smile faded and his eyes lit with desire. "Actually, I haven't. I've been craving something decadent and I only know one place to get it," he murmured, sliding his hand up her thigh.

The air surrounding them changed from playful to sizzling in a nanosecond. She didn't know who moved first, but they nearly tore each other's clothes off. Within a minute, they were both naked and she was straddling him on the couch. He palmed her face while his mouth plundered hers. She squirmed, trying to get closer, and he grasped her waist, lifted her and drove into her with one deep stroke, filling her completely. Maya cried out at the sweet invasion.

Ian muttered a curse and pulled out. "Wait...wait a minute." He reached for his discarded pants, found his wallet and dug out a condom.

She had totally forgotten about protection. Thank goodness one of them was thinking.

He sheathed himself and brought her down on him again. "Ride me, baby."

Holding on to his broad shoulders, she raised her body and eased back down, once, twice and a third time. She shivered and moaned when Ian captured a nipple between his lips and tugged gently.

"Ah, yes. The brown-sugar sweetness I've been wanting," Ian groaned.

Although Maya was on top, Ian dictated the pace, firmly holding her hips and moving with deep steady strokes. He thrust upward with every one of her downward strokes. She rode him faster and faster and he matched her pace, their moans filling the room. Ian locked his mouth on hers, reached between their bodies and teased her using his thumb, increasing the sensations. Sparks shot up her spine and she jerked her mouth free of his and screamed as an orgasm hit. Before she could recover, Ian bucked wildly beneath her.

"Maya!"

Their bodies shook and shuddered while they fought to catch their breaths. Maya collapsed against his chest and rested her head on his shoulder. *Reason number ten why I need to stay away from this man.*

At length, Ian asked, "Is it just me, or is it hot in here?"

She laughed softly. "Only in LA will you find eighty-degree temperatures in November." She rose and went to turn on the air conditioner. "I'll be right back. There's a bathroom right down that hall you can use," she added, gesturing in that direction.

Maya closed the door to her bedroom and lightly banged her head against it. "What are you doing, Maya Nicole Brooks?" As much as she enjoyed sex with Ian, she had to find a way to keep her emotions from coming into play. She had never been good at separating the two, but this time she would. Her heart depended on it.

Ian watched Maya's naked body until she was out of sight. His passions stirred to life. He flopped back against the sofa and closed his eyes. The air conditioner did nothing to cool him off. The more time he spent inside her body, the more he wanted. And he shouldn't want her this much. Sighing deeply, he came to his feet and went to wash up. When he came back, Maya still hadn't returned. He dressed and then surveyed the room. Upon his arrival, Ian had been so focused on Maya he hadn't taken more than a cursory glance around her place. Cream-colored walls and carpets— standard rental colors—but the blues and greens she had added gave the room a tropical feel. He noticed a stack of large boxes on the other side of the room. Was she moving?

"I'm ready."

He turned at the sound of Maya's voice. She now wore an off-the-shoulder pink top, a long skirt and short-heeled sandals. "Why did you change? I rather liked the first outfit."

"Ha-ha. That outfit does not leave the house."

"Yeah. You have a point." For some reason, he didn't want any other man seeing her in such revealing attire. "I like your place. Makes me think of a tropical island."

Maya angled her head and crossed her arms. "Most men wouldn't notice things like that."

"I'm an architect, remember? I notice things most men wouldn't," he added pointedly. He gestured toward the boxes. "Are you moving?"

"No. Those are my Christmas decorations."

"There are seven boxes over there. Are you decorating the entire complex?"

Maya laughed. "Of course not. But I *love* Christmas. I collect angel ornaments, so two of the boxes are just for them. My Christmas music playlist is ready with 'Silent Night' by The Temptations at the top." She shrugged. "It's my favorite time of the year and I get a little out of control."

He shook his head. "I'd say so."

She placed her hands on her hips. "Don't tell me you're a Scrooge."

Ian chuckled. "No, but I don't typically decorate. I live alone and can't see spending all that money on decorations no one will see."

"Do you live in a house, condo or apartment?"

"House. Why?"

"Then lots of people will see your decorations when they drive by. You don't have an excuse. When I buy a house, I plan to go all out—lights, snow..."

"Like those pimped-out houses featured on TV?" A huge grin blossomed on her beautiful face and she nodded. Ian couldn't help getting caught up in her excitement. "That I'd like to see. And where would you get snow from?"

"I'd love to drive up to Big Bear and bring some back, but, depending on the weather, it would probably melt within a few hours, so I'll have to settle for the fake stuff in the stores. You said you're an architect. Are there any notable buildings with your signature on them?"

Ian smiled. "Not yet, but soon hopefully. I have designed a few smaller buildings."

"Your house?"

"No, but I did do my brother's. He wanted it as a gift for his wife."

"That's so sweet. Maybe I'll get you to design my house one day."

"Maybe. So, where would you like to go for dinner?"

Maya shrugged. "Doesn't matter. What do you have a taste for?"

Ian lifted his brow a fraction. He threw his head back and roared at her embarrassed expression when she realized what she'd asked.

"Um…there's a Mexican restaurant not far. We can go there. Let me get my purse. I'll be right back," she mumbled, and exited like the room was on fire.

Still chuckling, he wondered if she knew just how close she had come to being on the menu tonight. *Looks like it might be a great holiday after all.*

Thursday morning, Rhonda breezed into the kitchen, snagged a still-warm cinnamon roll and came over to the stove, where Maya stood. "You're never smiling at six thirty in the morning. What gives?"

Maya looked up from the raspberry sauce she was stirring. "Morning, Rhonda. As I recall, you're the one who's not a morning person. And what's wrong with smiling?"

Rhonda eyed Maya. "Nothing, but we have a meeting with that man from the developer's company this afternoon and you were pretty upset yesterday when we closed. So what happened between then and now? Did they pull the offer?"

"I wish," she said with a roll of her eyes. "Ian stopped by my house last night."

"*Ian?* How did he get your address?"

"Apparently, when I gave the chef at the Bonaventure my contact information—smart me had left my cards in the car—I wrote down my home address. I told him he was free to share it with prospective clients. I'll have to go back and give him the shop's address."

Rhonda sighed wistfully. "A determined man. I wish stuff like that would happen to me. So?"

"Against my better judgment, I agreed to our original agreement. The man does not play fair," she said, recalling the way she had ridden him last night on her couch.

"That look on you face tells me, fair or not, he plays well."

"Yeah, he does. But I need to get my mind off Ian and on the meeting this afternoon. I'm not looking forward to it, because I know it won't be the end."

Later, after closing, Maya sat in her office thinking about her meeting with the man from EJJ Developers. Just as she predicted, he was not happy when she wouldn't entertain the offer for her property. The price he quoted was above the building's market value and more than she had paid, but none of that mattered. Saving her business did. And as much as she wished she could wave a magic wand and make this all go away, Maya knew she hadn't heard the last of the developer. Her cell chimed. Picking it up from the desk, she read a text message from Ian: I want to see you tonight. Her first thought was to reply with a resounding yes, but the rational part of her warned against letting him get too close. After several minutes of inner debate, she typed back: Can't. Need to work late to prepare for a party. It was partly true. She did have to provide desserts for a client tomorrow. The cell chimed again.

Ian: R u free Saturday night?

Maya: Yes.

Ian: Good. Can't wait to kiss you again. I'll bring the melted chocolate. I just need you to provide that brown sugar sweetness I can't get enough of.

Her pulse jumped. Warm chocolate, more of his expert kisses and extraordinary bedroom skills… She was in so much trouble.

Chapter 6

"This woman is driving me crazy!" Chris stormed into Ian's office, closing the door forcefully.

Ian turned from his drafting table. "Shellie finally realized that she could do better?"

Chris snorted. "Of course not. My wife knows there is no other man for her. I'm talking about the woman who's holding up the condo project."

"She still won't sell?" he asked incredulously.

"No. We offered more than the fair market value and she won't budge. It's been two weeks since Sam went to her shop. He's called twice and she basically told him not to bother calling again."

Ian blew out a long breath. "I need this deal to go through. What are we going to do?"

Chris propped a hip against the table and folded his arms. "Dad is going to try to schedule a meeting with her for the first or second week of December. Since today is Thursday and Thanksgiving is next week, he thought it would be better to hold off."

"It must be serious if Dad's going to hold the meeting."

"He doesn't want to mess around with this. Apparently, word got back to him that a couple of the investors from Capshaw's party are getting antsy. Hopefully, she'll come around. I don't want this to mess up the holidays. You should plan on coming. We might need you."

Ian nodded. "I'll do whatever it takes to get this done. Just tell me when."

"Good." Chris angled his head and studied the design on the table. "Is that for the office complex?"

"Yeah. I want to have two or three designs ready, based on what the client requested. I'm ready to take on more projects, but Dad still seems reluctant. The other three architects will be doing the same and I want mine to stand out."

"Well, judging from these, I'd say you've pretty much got the deal locked up. And don't worry about Dad. He knows how good you are at your job. Oh, before I forget, Shellie said you're invited for dinner tonight."

Ian smiled. "As much as I love my sister-in-law's cooking, I'll have to take a rain check. Maya and I are hanging out tonight."

Chris's brow knit in confusion. "Maya?"

"Yep. The woman from the party."

"You're still seeing her? I thought it was supposed to be a one-nighter. It's been two weeks."

Yeah. Two weeks of the best sex of Ian's life. Visions of their lovemaking last Saturday popped into his head. "We agreed to a short-term affair just until the end of the year."

"And you're sure you'll be able to walk away after that time?"

He shrugged. "Why wouldn't I? I'm not looking for anything long-term and neither is she." Somewhere in the back of his mind, a nagging voice told him walking away might not be as easy as he thought, but he immediately dismissed it. Ian glanced down at his watch, stood, shut down his laptop and rolled up the papers. "I need to get going."

"For a casual affair, you sure are eager to see her. And on a weeknight," Chris said with a smile. "You've never acted this way with other women."

"How do you know?" Ian asked, making sure to lock up his files. He was taking his designs home to work on them...if his evening with Maya ended early.

"Remember, I've been around since you were born. So I know you pretty well." Chris followed Ian out of the office and waited while he locked the door. "Sounds to me like things are not as casual as you'd like to believe." He clapped Ian on the shoulder. "Have fun and don't forget what I told you at the party." He strolled off down the hall to his office without waiting for a reply.

He ignored Chris's reference to being bitten by the love bug. Ian had no intention of being bitten by anything. But no matter what he tried to tell himself, he enjoyed being with her. His anticipation mounted the closer he got to Maya's place. And by the time he rang her doorbell, his heart was racing with excitement. She greeted him with a smile that made his heart leap.

"Hi, Ian. Come on in."

The greeting was barely off her tongue before he lifted her in his arms, kicked the door closed and kissed her with a hunger that stunned him and gave him pause. He eased back and lowered her to the floor.

"Now, *that's* a greeting," Maya said, taking his hand and leading him to the living room. "It was your turn to pick the place for dinner, so what did you decide?"

"Actually, I was thinking we could stay in tonight—pick up something to eat and take it back to my place." Where in the hell had that come from? Ian had never invited a woman he was casually dating to his house, and he tried to figure out a way to rescind the offer.

Maya's eyes lit up and she smiled brightly. "That's a great idea. I don't really feel like going to a restaurant. But I wish you would've told me earlier so I could make dessert."

Her smile and enthusiasm, along with the mention of her desserts, killed any notion he had of reneging. "Don't worry about it. We can always get dessert later, if you want."

She waved him off. "Wait a minute while I check the kitchen. I usually keep a little something, just in case. Can I get you something to drink?"

"Just some water please."

"Okay." She started to the kitchen, then turned back. "And I know you like chocolate."

As soon as she was out of sight, Ian scrubbed a hand down his face and groaned. What was he thinking?

"I'm ready."

He spun around at the sound of Maya's voice. His gaze strayed to the small gift bag in her hand. "You made a dessert already?" he asked, taking a bottle of water from her outstretched hand. He unscrewed the cap and took a huge gulp.

She shook her head. "No. I had some chocolate-chip cookie dough in the freezer. They'll only take about fifteen minutes. But, if you don't mind, I can pop them in the oven at your place."

Ian nearly choked on the water going down his throat. He coughed and tried to catch his breath. *Cook? At his place?* Granted, he had a state-of-the-art kitchen, but he had never allowed any woman, including his ex, at his stove. That implied an intimacy he purposely avoided.

"Are you okay?" Maya asked with concern.

He nodded. "Fine, fine. Just swallowed wrong." He composed himself and took a small sip of water.

"You sure?"

"Yeah."

"So, about the cookies…here or your place?"

He stared at her for a lengthy minute. "We can do them at my place." He'd already invited her over and it would seem rude to have her bake them here. Or at least that was what he told himself.

They agreed upon and ordered from an Italian restaurant. On the drive to Ian's house, Maya sat quietly thinking about the invitation to his house. Frankly, she was a little surprised, given the nature of their relationship. Most men didn't invite women into their homes unless… She quickly struck the thought from her mind. No. They agreed. Just through the holidays. A hand on her thigh interrupted her thoughts.

"You okay?"

"Yes. Why?"

"You're quiet. You mentioned not wanting to go out. Is anything wrong?"

"No. Just some work stuff. Nothing I can't handle." She hadn't heard anything from the real estate company since she'd declined their last offer almost two weeks ago, but knew they weren't going to back off. The thought of losing her dream weighed heavily on her mind. Not wanting to dwell on that prospect, she asked Ian, "What about your job—do things slow down for you over the holidays?"

"Sometimes, but this year we're hoping to get a project off the ground soon," Ian answered, turning into a cul-de-sac.

Maya's complex was located in a nice neighborhood, but Ian's home was in one of the more expensive areas—immaculate lawns, large stately houses with balconies, two-and three-car garages. He pulled into the third driveway. "Wow, this is fabulous."

"Thanks." He got out, retrieved their food from the backseat and then came around to her side.

She stared at the large two-story structure as they headed up the walkway. The house was impressive, even in the dark. He unlocked the door, stepped back for her to enter and touched a light switch. "Very nice," she said, glancing around the large foyer and into the living room to the right—polished wooden floors, dual staircase, and elegant and expensive furniture.

"Come on back to the kitchen," Ian said.

"This kitchen is amazing. I'd love to have one this size for all the baking I do."

He chuckled. "Do you want to bake the cookies now or later?"

"Now is fine. Can you preheat the oven to three hundred and fifty degrees?"

He placed the bags on the kitchen table, set the oven, and got plates and silverware. "Would you like a glass of wine?" Ian pulled out a small cookie sheet and handed it to her.

"Sure." She arranged the cookies on the sheet and slid the tray into the oven.

He retrieved and opened a bottle of pinot grigio from

a small wine cellar containing half a dozen bottles, seated her at the table and took the chair across from her.

They ate in silence for a few minutes and then Maya asked, "What made you go into architecture? I remember you telling me you loved to draw, but was there something else?"

"When I was eight, one of my neighbors' houses burned down. I was fascinated with the rebuild. Every day, when I came home from school, I would get as close as I could and watch. I wondered how they knew where to place each piece of wood, how they knew which room was which and the sizes…everything." He smiled as if remembering. "The architect happened to be there one of those afternoons and he, surprisingly and patiently, answered the million and one questions I had, showed me blueprints. Even gave me his card."

"That is so cool."

"Yeah. After that, I was always in my room working on some great masterpiece. Told my parents I was going to design the biggest building in Los Angeles."

Maya laughed. "And have you?"

"Not yet, but I'm working on it."

The timer on the oven went off and Maya removed the cookies, put them on a plate to cool and came back to the table to finish her dinner.

"Do you want something else?" Ian asked when they were done.

"No, thank you. This was some of the best seafood Alfredo I've ever had."

He stood, topped off their glasses of wine and picked up the plate of cookies. "Let's take this into the family room."

She followed him and settled onto the buttery-soft black leather sofa. She surveyed the room. Two matching recliners flanked the sofa and a large flat-screen TV was mounted on the wall above the fireplace in front of them. A bar with three stools occupied the other side of the room.

"I was trying to let my food digest before trying one of the cookies, but I can't wait," Ian said, reaching for one. He bit into it and groaned. "This is so good. I could eat all of these in one sitting."

She smiled, secretly thrilled about his praise for her desserts. She laughed as he devoured four of the twelve she had baked in a matter of minutes.

"Okay. I need to stop." He picked up a remote and pressed a button, and music floated through the room. "Come dance with me." He stood and pulled Maya to her feet.

She recognized the distinctive sound of Kem's voice immediately. She wrapped her arms around Ian's neck and leaned her head against his shoulder. They swayed slowly as Kem sang "Human Touch."

"I know you told me last weekend how many hours a day you spend baking, but how do you come up with your recipes?"

"Some of them are family recipes. Others are twists on familiar recipes or me just mixing ingredients together and experimenting."

"Obviously, you're doing something right. I haven't tasted one bad thing."

"Thank you." Ian was the first man she had dated who seemed genuinely interested in her career. He was making it hard to keep her guard up. Relaxing and dancing with him in this intimate environment didn't help, either.

"I don't think I ever asked and it wasn't on the card

the chef gave me, but do you have a name for your business?"

"You haven't and yes I do... Maya's Sweet Spot."

Ian stopped dancing. "It's a perfect name."

She lifted her head and met his eyes.

"I can think of several sweet spots on your body, starting here," he murmured, nibbling on her neck.

Her breath caught.

"And here."

The feel of his warm mouth skating across her chest woke every nerve in her body and she moaned softly. Maya knew she should slow things down, say something... anything. She needed to keep her barriers.

"Oh, and I can't forget about here," he said, slanting his mouth over hers in a passionate and intoxicating kiss. Caressing her face, he said, "In fact, I'd like to reacquaint myself with every sweet spot on your body. And search out a few more."

The desire burning in his eyes and seductive proposal tempted her beyond reason. He swept her into his arms and reclaimed her mouth. Each stroke of his tongue weakened her resolve until she could do nothing except yield to the pleasure. Her body wanted this. She only hoped her heart didn't follow.

Chapter 7

Dressed in a T-shirt and shorts, Ian padded barefoot downstairs Saturday morning to his kitchen, pressed the button on his single-serve coffeemaker brewing system and went out to retrieve the newspaper. Thanksgiving was still five days away, yet one of his neighbors had his lawn filled with boxes, strings of lights, large bows and a host of other Christmas decorations. The sight made him think of Maya. By the time he came back to the kitchen, his coffee was ready. He added sugar, sat at the bar and took a sip.

Her enthusiasm about Christmas brought a smile to his face, as did remembering their time in his home two nights ago. The more time he spent with her, the more he wanted to be with her. He was even contemplating shopping for Christmas decorations and a tree. Maybe she would help him decorate. His smile faded and he lowered the cup to the counter. What the hell was he thinking making plans as if they were a real couple? They weren't. He'd never had a problem separating the physical from the emotional, but this time he was fighting hard to maintain his distance. He shook his head, opened the paper and lifted the cup again. His phone rang. He set the cup down, reached across the bar for the phone and checked the display.

"Morning, Mom," he said after connecting.

"Good morning. Are you busy?"

Ian paused. "Ah, no," he answered slowly. Any time his mother started the conversation with that question meant trouble.

"Oh, good. I'm getting a head count for Thanksgiving dinner and wanted to know if you might be bringing a lady friend. Chris mentioned you were seeing someone."

He planned to strangle his brother on sight. Chris, of all people, knew the details of Ian and Maya's relationship, one that did *not* include family dinners.

"Is she a nice girl?" his mother asked excitedly.

"No, wait, yes, but she's not—" He searched his mind for the right words to explain his relationship with Maya. It wasn't like he could tell his mother the truth— that he and Maya were only having a sexual relationship. Yet he felt the stirrings of something more. No. He didn't want anything more. Wouldn't put his heart out there again. Then why couldn't he stop wanting her?

"Ian!"

His mother's annoyed voice snapped him out of his inner debate. "I'm sorry. What did you say?"

She sighed impatiently. "I asked whether you were bringing your lady friend."

"No. It's not that kind of relationship. So who's coming?" he asked, hoping to distract her from further questions.

She rattled off a list of relatives and close friends. "Then what kind of relationship is it?"

Ian smothered a groan. "We're just friends and I'm sure she'll be spending the day with her family. I have to get going, Mom. There are a few drawings I need to go over."

"You're not getting any younger, Ian, and don't you see how happy your brother is?"

He pinched the bridge of his nose. "Mom, Shellie is a great woman and she's perfect for Chris. I'm sure the perfect woman will come along sometime in the distant future. I just want to keep my focus on all the things going on at the office for now."

"Well, that's progress. Last time you said it would never happen. How are you coming with that big project?"

Did I just say that? "So far, so good, except there's one business owner who doesn't want to sell. Hopefully, she'll come around soon."

"Your father mentioned he's planning to bring you in for the meeting in a couple of weeks. Well, if anyone can change her mind it's you."

"Thanks, Mom."

"I'll see you next week, baby. Love you."

"Love you, too, Mom."

Ian disconnected, got his coffee and headed for the room he had set up as an office. He took a seat at his drafting table, picked up the drawing he had started of the senior living complex and added more details. Nowadays designs could be done almost exclusively on the computer, but he still preferred to draw his by hand first. Minutes later, his mind went back to Maya. He tried to push the thoughts aside and focus on his task but gave up after several minutes. He buried his head in his hands. She was getting to him.

He went to his bedroom for socks and tennis shoes, then headed for his small home gym. He hoped the physical exertion would curb his desire for Maya. After an hour, the only thing exhausted was his body. Thoughts of Maya continued to dominate the space in his mind, but he was determined to ignore them. Ian toyed with going out for a swim in the pool, but nixed the idea, since the temperatures had dropped by a good fifteen degrees over the last two days.

He spent the remainder of the day working in his office, stopping only to eat. As he lay in bed that night, memories of making love to Maya and her lingering presence in his room surfaced and filled him with a longing he was helpless to fight. Ian decided that tomorrow—distance be damned—he had to see her.

Sunday afternoon, the moment Maya opened the door and smiled at him, sensations he couldn't describe swirled in the pit of his stomach. He had called her earlier and asked if he could come over.

"Hey," Maya said. "Come on in. Let me get my purse and list, and then we can go."

He followed her inside and closed the door behind him. "List? Exactly how much stuff do you plan to buy? You said you only needed a few items." He had agreed to go shopping with her, which was a testament to how badly he wanted to see her. Ian only shopped out of necessity.

"I do, but I always make a list so I don't forget anything," she called over her shoulder.

What had he gotten himself into? She came back a moment later and he led her out to his car. Once en route, he asked, "Why are you shopping for Christmas decorations so early?"

"Actually, this is late for me."

His eyes left the road briefly to glance at her incredulously.

She laughed. "I put up my decorations the day after Thanksgiving. December tends to be really busy with all the holiday parties, and if I don't do it now, I may not get around to it. Hopefully, I can find everything in one store."

Ian felt his eyes widen. "Do you typically find what you're looking for in one spot?"

"Nope. Most times I end up at six or seven places."

He swallowed hard and tried to keep the panic out of his voice. "You don't plan on going to that many stores today, do you?"

"Of course not. I know most men would rather endure a root canal than go shopping, so I won't torture you. Whatever I don't find today, I'll get tomorrow after I'm done baking."

Thank goodness! "Okay. You mentioned being busier next month. Have you booked many events?" They only had a month left, and for some reason, knowing he might not see her much didn't sit well with him.

"Yes. I have something every week through New Year's. I also have two clients this week for Thanksgiving."

"You're working on Thanksgiving?"

"No. They'll pick up the day before."

"Do you make the desserts for your family, too?"

"Thankfully, no. My mother, aunt and grandmother take care of it. Every year, I have a hard time not jumping in to help. But one look from my grandmother sends me running. What about you? Do you have family here?"

"Yes. We all get together at my parents' house. My mother and several aunts put out a feast. The guys are responsible for the cleanup." He parked in the Cost Plus World Market lot, got out and came around to her side. They walked hand in hand to the store entrance.

"That's a great idea," she said, continuing the conversation. "I think I'll mention it to my mom. She'll *love* it." Maya chuckled. "My dad, on the other hand, probably won't."

"My dad and uncles weren't too keen on the idea, either…until the women threatened to go on strike. Brought them right around." They both laughed. "Wow, there's a lot of stuff in here." Ian glanced around and saw everything from china and flatware to soaps and pillows. He hadn't a clue as to how she would be able to find what she needed…or how long he would have to be in the store. Maya picked up a small basket and moved through the store like a woman with a purpose and seemed to know exactly where she was going. She selected two silver baskets, a set of silver candles and blue candleholders. As they walked toward the back, he noted a wall of wines and a variety of coffees, teas and food.

"Since we're here, you should get some stuff to decorate your house," Maya said.

Ian turned to face her. "I don't know."

"Oh, come on. Don't be such a party pooper," she teased. "You can't tell me being in this store hasn't put you into the holiday spirit."

"Are you coming to help me decorate?" He couldn't tell who was more surprised as the words left his mouth.

"Um…sure, if you want me to."

They stood in awkward silence for a few moments. "There are a couple of angel ornaments over there." He gestured and quickly walked over to an ornament display and picked up a set of two gold glitter angels with a gem head.

She joined him and smiled. "I bought similar ones last year. I have a glass one and a set of three silver-plated ones. Among several others."

He shook his head and continued to follow her around as she shopped. Before he knew it, they had gone back for a cart and filled it with decorations for his house. By the time they returned to her house, Ian was more confused than ever about his feelings.

"You can just put those bags by the fireplace with the boxes," Maya said, entering her condo.

He placed the bags where she indicated and came back to help remove her jacket.

She took it from him and draped it over the back of a chair. "Do you want something to drink?"

"No. The only thing I want is to kiss you." Ian gathered her in his arms and stared into her eyes, trying to understand why he wanted her so much. He lowered his head and touched his mouth to hers, then captured her lower lip and sucked gently. Her lips parted and his tongue found hers. He kissed her slowly, deeply, feeding from the sweetness within. She moved closer to him and molded her body against his. He shuddered. Suddenly, an emotion unlike anything he had ever experienced spread throughout his chest. He broke off the kiss. "I'd better get going. I have some work to finish for a meeting tomorrow morning."

Maya stared up at him, seemingly confused. "Okay."

He donned his jacket, took her hand and walked to the door. "I'll talk to you later." Unable to resist, he kissed her once more and slipped out the door. In his car, Ian leaned back against the headrest and closed his eyes. His heart thumped hard in his chest and beads of perspiration dotted his forehead. *What is going on?* The feelings coursing through his body scared the hell out of him. He glanced down at his hands, which were trembling. Taking a deep breath, Ian willed himself calm. It was nothing, he assured himself. Just getting caught up in the holiday spirit brought on from shopping. He'd be back to normal in a couple of hours.

Except he wasn't back to normal hours later. In fact, four days later, his emotions were still running high. Because of her schedule, he and Maya had been playing phone tag all week and had merely exchanged a few texts. Normally, when it came to women, that old adage "out of sight, out of mind" worked perfectly for him. This time, his feelings for her were steadily intensifying despite the lack of communication.

During Thanksgiving dinner, Ian couldn't help noticing the heated looks, subtle touches and secret smiles that passed between his brother and sister-in-law. Chris seemed…content. He glanced around the dining room table and saw the same contentment reflected in the faces of his parents, aunts and uncles, and two of his cousins who were married. For the first time, Ian felt a twinge of jealousy. He toyed with the food on his plate, his appetite rapidly waning, and was more than happy when dinner ended.

"You all right, Ian?" Chris asked when they were alone in the kitchen.

"Yeah, why?"

"You're quieter than usual and you didn't have seconds."

Ian shrugged. "I wanted to save room for dessert."

"That's never stopped you before."

"I just have a lot on my mind with work, that's all."

Chris scrutinized Ian for a lengthy minute. "I see. So, how's Maya?"

"I guess she's fine. I haven't talked to her since Sunday."

"And you're miserable as hell," he said with a chuckle.

"Why would I be miserable? I keep telling you it's not that kind of relationship."

"If you say so. I'm going to get dessert. You coming?"

"In a minute, after I empty the trash."

Chris nodded and left the kitchen.

Ian stared after Chris until the door closed. He braced his hands on the counter and bowed his head. His brother was spot-on, but he had no intention of saying so. Releasing a deep breath, he grabbed up the trash bag. Maya was coming over to help him decorate on Sunday, which gave him three days to get his head back on straight.

Sunday afternoon, Maya parked in Ian's driveway and shut off the engine. Before she made it up the walkway, the door swung open and Ian stood there barefoot, wearing jeans and a T-shirt that molded to his magnificent physique. He unleashed a smile that warmed her all over.

"Hey. Come in." He kissed her and closed the door. "What's in the bag?"

She held up the bag. "I made truffles for a bridal shower. I thought you might like some, so I made a few extra."

He placed his hand on his chest. "A woman after my own heart."

His heart. Was she really after his heart? Although his words were teasing, a tiny part of her wished she did have his heart. She went still.

"Maya?"

She shook her head to clear the errant thought and extended the bag. "So," she said brightly, "are you ready to decorate?"

Ian took the bag, still staring at her curiously. "Yeah. Let me run upstairs and get my shoes and a sweatshirt first. Make yourself comfortable. I'll be right back."

"Okay." As soon as he was gone, Maya covered her mouth in disbelief and paced the floor. Maybe helping Ian decorate was a bad idea. They were behaving like a real couple—the shopping, hand-holding, laughter, decorating—and it was getting to her. All week she'd been wrestling with her growing feelings and she had no idea how to make them stop.

"All right, let's get these lights up outside."

She whirled around at the sound of Ian's voice. "I don't remember you buying any lights."

"I picked them up this week," he said, leading her out to the garage. He pressed a wall switch and two of the three garage doors lifted. "I figured I might as well add the lights, since you talked me into getting those lighted lawn structures."

She helped him carry everything out to the front and waited while he went back for a ladder. Over the next three hours, they strung the lights, arranged and rearranged the lighted lawn decorations. It was near dusk when they finished.

"I think we're done," Ian said. "Be right back." He jogged to the garage, plugged in the lights and jogged back.

"*Wow!* It's beautiful." Maya took in the sight of all

the twinkling white icicle lights bordering the first and second levels, and the single white lights framing the large picture window.

Ian joined her at the curb and slung an arm around her shoulder. "It does look good, huh?" He turned her face toward his and tilted her chin. "Thank you," he whispered just before taking her mouth in a long, drugging kiss. "Your lips are cold. Let's get you inside and warm you up."

Maya shivered from his kiss as much as from the cold. She followed him inside to the kitchen and slid onto a barstool.

"I made chicken soup and thought we could have that and turkey sandwiches."

"You made soup? From scratch?"

He chuckled. "Yes, but I took a couple of shortcuts. I used store-bought chicken stock, and sautéed the vegetables to give it that simmered-all-day flavor."

"I'll have to remember that the next time I make chicken soup." She laughed and hopped down from the stool. "I need to wash my hands."

"I'll have everything ready in a few minutes." He directed her to the kitchen table when she returned and it wasn't long before he brought bowls of soup and plates with the sandwiches over.

"Mmm, this smells delicious."

Ian took the seat at the head of the table. "Hopefully, you'll say the same thing about the taste."

Maya spooned up a portion, blew on it for a few seconds to cool it, then put it in her mouth. "This is really good."

"Thanks." They ate in silence for a while. "I have one more decorating project I'd like you to help me with before you leave."

"What's that?"

"My tree."

"Wow, you're really going all out," she said with a smile.

Ian reached for her free hand and stared intently at her. "You inspired me."

The tender look in his eyes rendered her mute momentarily, but she quickly recovered and gently pulled her hand from his. "Aw, I'm glad. That's what friends are for," she added to lighten the mood. They completed the meal while conversing. After cleaning up, he led her into the formal living room, where a live tree at least eight feet tall stood. Boxes of ornaments had been neatly stacked beside it.

Ian rubbed his hands together. "Shall we?" He handed her one box and opened another.

As they hung ornament after ornament, once again, the intimate atmosphere caused an inner turmoil and made her wish for something beyond their original agreement.

"Here, I saved the last one for you."

Maya opened the box and found a beautiful angel tree topper—angelic brown face, silver gown, lace bodice adorned with pearls and shimmering sequins, and cascading organza ribbon.

"I know how much you love angels."

She was in deep, deep trouble. With his help, she climbed the ladder, placed the angel in her spot, climbed down and waited while he lit the tree. "It's lovely."

"I couldn't agree more," he whispered.

Maya turned to find his gaze locked on her.

"One last touch." He produced a small cellophane package from behind his back and held it up.

"Is that…?"

"Yep. Gotta have a little mistletoe." Ian lowered his head. "Maya," he murmured against her lips, "will you help me christen my tree?"

Her mind screamed *no!* But her body answered with a resounding yes. He undressed them both and drew her down to the carpet in front of the tree. When he kissed her again, she locked her arms around his neck and forgot about everything except the pleasure he was giving her.

Chapter 8

A week later, Maya put the final touches on the chocolate torte and packed it, along with a strawberry cheesecake and the individual three-layer red velvet cake slices the host wanted for each of her dinner guests. She stifled a yawn brought on by another night of restless sleep. She hadn't slept well since the night she and Ian made love in front of his Christmas tree. Everything about that night was different. Their lovemaking was no less intense, but the way he touched and kissed her felt different. And when their eyes locked…she knew she had fallen in love with him. Maya braced her hands on the table in front of her. How could she have allowed her emotions to get involved? She had lain awake every night asking herself the same question and wondering how to keep him from finding out.

"Hey, girl. You just about ready?" Rhonda asked, breezing into the room.

"I just need to add the rest of these cake slices."

"I know there's an extra piece, right?"

"Yes, Rhonda. You only asked about it ten times," Maya said with a laugh, closing the container. "Help me load this in my car and you can get your cake."

"Gladly." Rhonda picked up one storage container and Maya grabbed the other. "Are we still on for dinner tomorrow night or do you and Ian have another hot Saturday night planned?" she asked with a giggle.

"Yes, we're still on. We have that meeting with EJJ Development on Monday and I want to be prepared." She couldn't afford a distraction right now, and Ian was definitely a huge one. She and Rhonda were going to work on a strategy over dinner tomorrow night.

"I don't know how we're going to fight this, Maya," she said with a deep sigh, placing the container in the back of Maya's SUV.

"I don't know, either. But I *do* know that I'm not going to lie down and let them run roughshod all over me." She was trying to remain positive but knew she faced an uphill battle.

"I hear you. Anyway, how are things with Ian?"

"Okay, I guess," Maya said nonchalantly. But Rhonda could read her like a book.

Rhonda studied Maya, then brought her hands to her mouth. "Oh, my God. You've fallen for him, haven't you?"

She dropped her head and heaved a deep sigh. "I don't know what I'm going to do. This wasn't supposed to happen."

"Does he know?"

Her head snapped up. "Of course not. What we have will be over at the end of the month. He doesn't want anything past that and neither do I."

"Are you sure? I know you were hurt before, but—"

"No *buts*. This was nothing more than a holiday fling, and that's all it will be."

"What about him? Are you certain he doesn't want more?"

Her mind went back to their last encounter. No, she wasn't sure, but she didn't want to take a chance. "It doesn't matter." Maya closed the hutch. "I'd better get going. I'll see you in the morning."

"Okay. I'll lock up…after I get my cake, that is."

She chuckled and the two women embraced. "Bye, crazy woman."

"Bye, and you need to think twice about shutting Ian down cold. From what you've told me, he sounds like a nice guy."

"Whatever," she mumbled, rolling her eyes and getting into the car. Yeah, he was a nice guy, and so much more than what she had been expecting when she met him a month ago.

Ian called on Sunday and wanted to come over. She knew there would be no way to hide her feelings, so she let it go to voice mail. By the next morning, Maya still had no clue how to deal with her feelings. Every moment they had spent together played over and over in her mind, particularly the last time. Something had changed between them—from the possessive way he'd held her to the way he'd tenderly washed her body when they had showered—and the shift was palpable. *Stop thinking about him! You have more important things to focus on…like saving your business.*

Forcing her mind back to the task in front of her, she filled gift-box molds with melted chocolate and placed them on a shelf in the walk-in freezer. The boxes would be decorated with FDA-approved, food-grade edible luster dust and pearls, and filled with chocolate truffles for wedding shower gifts. Next, she made dough for cinnamon rolls. The shop would open in two hours, and the rolls were her bestselling product in the morning.

"So, I'm wondering, will the dough still rise if you keep beating it like that?" Rhonda's amused voice asked from the doorway.

Maya's hands froze. She glanced down and realized that she had been brutally attacking the dough. She began again, this time kneading the dough with a little less force.

"Are you worried about the meeting this afternoon or Ian?"

"A little of both, I guess."

"Ian is easy. See where the relationship goes." Rhonda came and placed her arm around Maya's shoulder. "I wish I could assure you we're going to come out winners this afternoon, but I'm worried, too. Last night, I did a little more research on eminent domain and I don't think they have a case."

"Maybe, but if the city sees a way to make big money, they won't care." She placed the dough in a bowl to rise and washed her hands. "I don't want to talk about it anymore. Four o'clock will be here soon enough."

"You're right. I would offer to help you bake, but..." She laughed. "How about I put the truffles in the chocolate boxes and package them? You'd think I had learned something after all these years of hanging around you, but hey...we all have our talents."

"Yeah, well," Maya said with a shrug. "I'll take any help I can get. Thanks."

The women worked steadily until opening time.

After the morning rush, Maya took a quick breather before prepping for her next event. She was so focused it took her a moment to realize her cell was ringing. She wiped her hands on a towel and hurried across the kitchen to catch it.

"Hey, baby," Ian said when she answered. "How's your day going?"

"Hey. Busy. Really busy." She hadn't looked at the display before answering.

"More catering jobs?"

"Yeah. I have two this week."

"Any chance we can get together later today? There's something I want to talk to you about."

Her heart rate kicked up. "It sounds important. What is it?"

"I don't want to say over the phone and yes, it's very important."

She glanced over at the wall clock. "It's eleven now. I may be able to meet you for a few minutes around two, unless something comes up. I have to get back for an appointment at four. Can I call you around one to let you know for sure?"

"That's fine. I have to go out to check on a work site, but I'll have my cell."

"Okay." She disconnected and tapped the phone against her chin. What was so important that he couldn't tell her over the phone? Was he ending their affair? The timer on the oven went off, drawing her out of her thoughts. "I'll find out soon enough."

Ian leaned back in his chair and rotated it toward the window. There was so much he wanted to say to Maya and he had to do it face-to-face. Somewhere along the way his feelings changed and she had slowly eased into his heart. He sensed it when they went shopping, but he knew for sure after they made love on his living room floor in front of the tree. It was the first one he had put up in the three years he'd lived in the house. He didn't want their affair to end. He wanted to talk to her about something more long-term. He checked his watch. Landon, one of the other architects, would be at Ian's office any minute to accompany Ian to the construction site of an office complex. He rose to his feet and walked over to retrieve his jacket just as a knock sounded.

"Perfect timing," he said, opening the door. "Chris. I thought you were Landon."

"You have a minute?"

"Not really. What's up?"

"I wanted to talk to you about the meeting this afternoon."

"Can it wait?"

"No."

Ian glanced around Chris's shoulder when Landon appeared in the door. "Well, it'll have to, big brother. Gotta go."

"Ian, wait. I think you should—"

He waved his brother off. "Whatever it is, I'll be ready for it. Be back later."

Out at the work site, he and Landon met with the construction foreman, walked through the building and compared the structure to the blueprints. Ian kept checking his watch, anxious to see Maya.

"Looks like we're on schedule. Excuse me a moment," he said when his cell rang. Ian walked a few steps away, checked the display and smiled upon seeing

Maya's name. "Hey, sweetheart. Where are we meeting?"

"I'm sorry, Ian, but I won't be able to meet you. My shipment was mistakenly left off the truck and I have to go to UPS to pick it up. I need it for tomorrow. Can we talk tomorrow?"

He ran a hand over his head and muttered a curse. "What about tonight? I can come to your house later."

"I have an appointment at four."

"I know. I have a late meeting at work, too. I can come by afterward. Six thirty?"

"All right. I have to go."

"I'll see you later."

"Ian?"

Ian spun around at the sound of Landon's voice.

"I think we might have a problem."

He stifled a groan. This was all he needed today.

By the time they made it back, Ian had five minutes to get cleaned up for the meeting with the lone holdout. He hurried to his office and used his private bathroom to change.

Chris met him on the way to the conference room. "Ian, there's something you should know before going in the meeting."

"You always say that," he joked. "I promise to be on my best behavior and bring out all the charm needed to get this deal done." He reached for the doorknob and Chris placed a staying hand on his arm. "Man, would you relax?" Ian said with a chuckle. "Now come on. We're already late." He opened the door and froze. His smile faded and his eyes widened when he saw the two women seated at the table. *No, no, no.* His stomach dropped. "Maya?" he whispered.

She slowly came to her feet. "Ian?"

Ian turned back and met his brother's grim expression. "Sorry, bro."

He turned back to Maya. Her expression went from shock to anger in a flash.

Ian's father cleared his throat. "Ah, Ms. Brooks, I see you've already met my youngest son, Ian. With him is my oldest son, Christopher. If you all take your seats we can get started."

Maya's angry gaze never left Ian's. "There's no need. Hell will freeze over before I sell you my shop," she gritted out. She snatched up her papers and purse and stormed past Ian out the still-open door.

Ian rushed after her. "Maya, wait." He reached out and caught her arm.

She snatched out of his grasp. "Don't touch me!"

"Maya, I'm sorry. I—"

"This is just another building to you, but it's *my life.* I will lose *everything*. You conspire to force me out of my business and the best you can do is *I'm sorry*? Are you sorry enough to drop this whole thing and let me keep my shop?"

His jaw tightened, but he remained silent.

"That's what I thought."

"Maya. I didn't know."

"And next you're going to tell me you knew nothing about this deal," she said sarcastically.

"Yes. Wait, no." Ian scrubbed an agitated hand down his face, took a deep breath and started again. "Yes, I knew about the deal. No, I didn't know your shop was the holdout."

"This whole relationship was one big lie." Maya chuckled mirthlessly. "So that was the important news.

At least now I know why you wanted to talk to me so bad." She turned and started down the hallway again.

The tears standing in her eyes were killing him. He stepped in front of her, blocking her path. "No, baby. That's not what I wanted to tell you. You have to believe me, Maya. I *didn't* know and nothing about our relationship has been a lie." He cradled her face between his palms. "I wanted to tell you, I love you. I love you, Maya."

She said nothing for several charged seconds, and for a brief moment her gaze softened before going cold again. "Nice try."

"I'm very serious. I do love you," he reiterated. Ian blew out another long breath. "I know you're really angry right now and I'm worried about you. Let me drive you home."

"I don't need anything from you, least of all your concern," she snapped. "Just stay away from me." She stepped around him and rushed down the hall.

This time he let her go. He stared after her, feeling like his heart was breaking. Ian let the wall take his weight, closed his eyes and banged his head softly against it. How could this happen?

"Mr. Jeffries?"

Ian opened his eyes and straightened from the wall. It was the woman who had sat next to Maya. She had smooth honey-brown skin, was tall, slender and moved with the grace of a model striding down a runway.

She extended her hand. "I'm Rhonda Davis, Maya's best friend and business partner."

"Call me Ian," he said, taking the proffered hand. "I'm sorry we have to meet under these circumstances." He pulled a business card from his pocket and handed it to her. "Can you please let mc know that Maya made it home safe? I'm concerned about her. I'd call myself, but right now I'm the last person she wants to talk to."

She studied him for a moment. "You've fallen in love with Maya, haven't you?"

"Yes. I just realized that I love her more than anything."

She hesitated, then took the card. "I'll see what I can do." She turned and walked away.

He stood in the hallway a moment longer before going back to the conference room.

"Looks like your relationship with Ms. Brooks is going to work in our favor," his father said as soon as Ian entered. "Your brother tells me you've been seeing her a few weeks."

"Yes."

"Good, good. Keep wooing her. Do whatever it takes to get this deal closed."

Ian shook his head. "I can't do that, Dad. I won't hurt her like that."

His father sat up in his chair. "What do you mean, you can't do it?" he gritted out. "You're going to let some woman you just met come between you and your obligation to this company? We've offered her almost twice what that shop is worth, so I don't understand her problem."

"Dad," Chris jumped in, "you know that's not fair."

Ian braced his hands on the desk. "Dad, you know as well as I do how hard it would be to start over if she has to move."

"This is about business. We can't afford to disappoint our investors. They've put up a lot of money and expect results."

"So has Maya," he countered. "Even with the amount we offered, she may not be able to recover her losses. Put yourself in her shoes. How would you feel if someone asked you to uproot your life?"

His father sighed heavily. "Ian, I understand what you're saying, but I don't see any way out for Ms. Brooks." He stood and walked to the door. "I'm sorry, son."

When the door closed behind his father, Ian slammed his hand on the table, spun around and let out a frustrated groan. "Why didn't you tell me, Chris?"

"I tried to tell you earlier, but you wouldn't listen. And before you jump down my throat, I only found out this morning when Sam dropped the file off in my office. I take it she's pretty mad."

"And hurt. She thinks I orchestrated the whole relationship to get her shop." He paced the room. "I love her, Chris. I can't make her lose her shop. It'll destroy her." He stopped, braced his hands on the table again and bowed his head. "I feel like this is a repeat of last time."

"This is nothing like last time, Ian. Laura tried to steal blueprints for her brother's company so they could win a bid. The only blueprint stolen this time was the one to your heart." He chuckled. "I guess I was right about that love bug biting you in the butt, huh?"

Ian angled his head and smiled faintly. "Guess so. But it doesn't matter now. If I close this deal I'll lose her for sure. If I help her keep it, I can kiss my career goodbye. Dad will have me stuck drawing closets for the rest of my life."

Chis placed a hand on Ian's shoulder. "You're one of the smartest people I know. If anybody can come up with a solution, it's you. I'll see you later."

He nodded. "Tell Shellie hello." Alone, Ian sank

into the closest chair and buried his head in his hands. Money notwithstanding, relocating meant that Maya couldn't take orders and would likely lose most of her clientele, and like she'd said, it could potentially destroy her business. He couldn't see any way out of this mess and didn't know what he was going to do. The only thing he knew for sure was that he couldn't...*wouldn't* let the woman he loved lose her livelihood.

Chapter 9

Maya dropped down on the sofa in her condo and swiped at the tears that hadn't stopped since she left the office complex. "There's no way I can survive a move, not in this economy. All my clients…"

Rhonda sat next to her and offered a box of tissues. "Are you going to be okay?"

She snatched out two tissues. "I'm about to lose my business and the man I foolishly fell in love with set me up. I'm just *great*."

"Sarcasm doesn't look good on you."

"I'm sorry," she said, leaning her head back against the couch. "It's not your fault that I keep finding losers." She let out a frustrated groan. "I can't believe he set me up like that. Everything, from the first night until now, was nothing more than an elaborate plan to get me to sell my building."

"For what it's worth, I don't think Ian knew it was your building. He seemed genuinely surprised."

"Yeah, right."

"No, seriously, Maya. His face registered the same shock as yours when he walked into that conference room. And he cares about you."

Maya glared at Rhonda. "Just whose side are you on? You're supposed to be *my* best friend."

Rhonda sighed. "You know I'm on your side, but the man is worried about you. He even wanted to make sure you got home okay."

She rolled her eyes. "It's all an act."

"You don't believe that any more than I do. I saw the way he looked at you. And he told me he loves you."

"I don't know what to believe right now." His declaration of love still resonated with her, but she wasn't sure if she could trust his words.

"On another note, you were right. He is definitely chiseled chocolate. His brother is just as fine. Do you know if he's single?"

She skewered Rhonda with a look.

"Okay, okay. Now's not the time. What are you going to do about Ian?"

"Nothing. We're done."

"Come on, Maya. Don't judge him too harshly. Like I said, I think he really cares about you. At the very least, give him a chance to explain." She shrugged. "You never know, he might be willing to help you."

"I don't want to talk about it anymore," she mumbled.

Rhonda gave Maya's hand an assuring squeeze and stood. "Things will work out. I'm going home. Call me if you need me."

Maya slowly came to her feet. "I'll be fine." She saw her friend to the door, then trudged down the hall to her bedroom. She should have stuck to her decision after that first night. Now, not only was everything she'd worked so hard to build in jeopardy, but she had also gotten her heart broken…again.

She moved around her shop the next morning in a haze. Sleepless nights and 4:00 a.m. days didn't go well together. She had ruined one batch of dough already, which put her behind schedule, and she tried to focus so as not to mess up the batch currently in front of her. After getting the cinnamon rolls in the oven, she made the custard for the fruit tarts and cupcakes for an elementary school class party that would be picked up later that morning.

"Morning, Ms. Brooks."

Maya stifled a groan. She had forgotten that the part-time culinary student she'd hired started today. "Hi, Phoebe." Twenty-two years old and barely five feet, Phoebe possessed a lively personality and enthusiasm for baking that had won Maya over immediately. Before Maya could say anything else, the young woman pulled a chef's jacket, hair net and toque from a tote bag. Maybe this was a good thing.

"What do you want me to do? I'm so excited about working with you. You make the most amazing chocolates."

She smiled. "Follow me." She put Phoebe to work and went out front to start filling the display cases. By the time she opened at seven, Maya was so impressed by the young woman that she considered hiring her permanently. That is, if she still had a place for her to work. Shaking off that negative thought, she put a smile on her face and greeted the first customers.

"Girl, it's busy in here today," Rhonda whispered two hours later as she passed Maya on the way to the register.

Maya was grateful for her customers and enjoyed

every moment of the sweat and tears she poured into Maya's Sweet Spot. The thought of it all going away caused a deep pain in her soul and she had to force down the emotions that threatened to rise again.

"Maya."

She whirled around. "What are you doing here?" she whispered. Ian stood on the other side of the counter wearing a navy suit, looking as good as he had the night they first met. Her traitorous body reacted to his nearness almost immediately.

"I had to make sure you were okay."

Maya wanted nothing more than to jump over the counter and into his arms. Determined not to let him see how much he affected her, she said, "I'm fine."

"That makes one of us," he murmured before glancing around the shop. "I see your decorating skills extend beyond your home. It's very festive and warm. I like the angel on the counter."

Ian moved closer to the counter and she instinctively moved back. Even with the display case between them, she could still feel his heat.

"I need to talk to you."

"I'm really busy."

"Baby, I just need five minutes. There are only three people in here right now and I'm sure Ms. Davis can handle things. Please," he added when she hesitated.

She peeked over her shoulder and found Rhonda viewing the exchange with mild amusement. "We can talk in my office." She led him back to her office, closed the door and waited for him to speak.

He came and placed his hands on her shoulders. "I know you think I engineered some kind of plan to seduce you into selling your building, but I didn't. I would never knowingly try to destroy your career. And, sweetheart, nothing about what we shared was fake. It's the most real thing in my life. I don't want what we have to end, Maya. I meant what I said yesterday and I'm going to keep saying it until you believe me. I love you. I love you more than anything and I promise I won't let you lose your dream, even if I have to build you another shop myself." He placed a small gift bag that she hadn't noticed he was carrying on her desk. "I know you have to get back to work. I'll see you later." He brushed his lips across hers and exited, closing the door softly behind him.

She wrapped her arms around her midsection and took several deep breaths to slow her heart rate. Even though she was still hurt, Ian had a way of getting to her. Turning slightly, Maya lifted the bag and took out a wrapped box. She carefully removed the paper and opened the plain brown box. Her breath caught. Inside was a carved wooden box with Maya's Sweet Spot engraved on the front. The moment she lifted the lid, her favorite Christmas song, "Silent Night"—not the typical windup music box version, but the version by The Temptations—began to play. She couldn't stop the tears from falling. He remembered. How was she going to let him go?

By the end of the week, Maya was beyond exhausted. She placed her purse and tote on the coffee table and collapsed on the sofa to open the package that had been left for her at the complex office. She hadn't ordered anything and didn't see a return address. She pulled out the attached note card and read: *An angel for my angel. Something to add to your collection.* Puzzled, she tore off the gift wrap and opened the box. "Oh, my," she whispered in awe. She couldn't believe it. Ian had sent her a Swarovski crystal angel ornament. She carefully removed it and placed it on her tree. The crystal caught the light and burst into a kaleidoscope of color. It was absolutely beautiful. She went back to the note. *His angel.* Her heart leaped. She hadn't seen or spoken to Ian since he walked out of her shop three days ago with his words of love and a promise to help her. Maya's gaze strayed back to the ornament again. She still wanted him...and loved him with every fiber of her being. She prayed the rest would work itself out.

Chapter 10

For the remainder of the week Ian divided his time between keeping up with his workload and researching a workable solution to the condo project. He searched websites for similar projects, trying to come up with something that would satisfy all parties, but he was unsuccessful. He also hadn't made any headway with Maya. She hadn't returned any of his calls since he walked out of her shop. He wanted to talk to her, touch her and hold her in his arms. He missed kissing her and yes, making love with her. As a result, he was frustrated, horny and miserable.

Ian leaned against the door frame of his living room staring at the Christmas tree and thinking about Maya's shop. It was small, but very functional and she had maximized her space. With her warm personality, she had created an inviting space. The architect in him could already visualize ways to expand the area to include a few tables and maybe a coffee and tea bar that would encourage customers to sit and enjoy her delectable pastries. She was also correct about it being located in the perfect spot. The combination of residential homes and commercial buildings, along with accessibility to the main highway, gave her a built-in clientele. It was one of the deciding factors when they chose that spot to house the condo project. Ensuring that the project went through would go a long way in boosting Ian's career. But advancing his career at the expense of hers was something he could not do. When he saw her that first night, the only thing on his mind had been the sex. He never planned on wanting her so completely. Never imagined falling in love. But he had. And he knew she loved him, too. He couldn't lose her.

Pushing off the wall, he headed to his home office. He was in for another long night, but Christmas was two weeks away and he was determined to spend it with Maya. Three hours later, still no closer to an answer, he stumbled from his office and fell across his bed fully clothed.

When he arrived at work the next morning, Ian needed a double shot of caffeine to get his mind working. He deposited his laptop bag and blueprints on his desk and headed directly down the hall to the coffee room. Fifteen minutes and one cup later, the haze around his brain began to clear. While he was searching the internet, an article caught his attention. He clicked on the link and started reading. His eyes moved rapidly across the screen. A smile curved his mouth and he hit the intercom.

"Yes, Mr. Brooks," his assistant answered.

"Ms. Smith, can you please set up an emergency meeting with all the investors on the Sutton Park condo project for Monday morning at eleven. Include my dad and Chris. When you're done, I need your help."

"I'll be in as soon as everything is set."

"Thank you." He hit the off button and rolled up his sleeves. He had a lot of work ahead of him but was confident he could pull it off.

Chris cornered Ian when he entered the conference room Monday morning. "What's going on?"

"Take a seat and you'll find out in a minute."

Chris eyed him skeptically, but Ian merely smiled and gestured for Chris to take a seat. He took a quick glance at the wall clock and called the meeting to order. "Good morning, ladies and gentlemen. Thank you for agreeing to meet on such short notice. I know you are all anxious to know why I called the meeting, so let's get started."

He waited a moment for his secretary to pass out the information packets, then turned on the projector. "There has been some concern about the one holdout on the Sutton Park project, and I believe I've come up with a way that will satisfy both parties. Your vision for this property is one of elegance and comfort. I'd like to add *convenience*. How many times have you forgotten something at the store and had to drive miles to get it?" Several people nodded. "What about going to the dry cleaner's?" He nodded at his secretary, who passed around plates holding a mini cinnamon roll and truffle. Ian smiled at the expressions of delight on each person's face as they all bit into the tasty treats. "And what if you were able to get these pastries and desserts every day?"

"Why, this truffle tastes like the ones I get from Maya's Sweet Spot," Mr. Capshaw said. "Ms. Brooks makes the best desserts around."

"I'm glad you feel that way, Mr. Capshaw. I'm not sure you knew this, but Maya's Sweet Spot was our holdout."

Mr. Capshaw's eyes widened.

Now that he had their attention, Ian flipped through the screens showing the redesigned property that included a minimarket, a dry cleaner's and a bakery. "Just think what it would mean to have Maya's breakfast goodies available within minutes of waking up." He continued citing the advantages, and by the time he finished, the group voted unanimously in favor of the new design.

Ian had scaled one hurdle, but the most important one was yet to come. The text he had been waiting for came an hour later. He walked down the hall to his father's office. "Dad, I need to leave for the rest of the afternoon."

"I'm proud of you, son. I wasn't sure you could pull it off, but you were brilliant. Going to celebrate?" he asked with a chuckle.

"Not quite. I have a more personal matter."

His father's brow lifted. "This wouldn't have anything to do with Ms. Brooks, would it?"

Ian grinned. "Yes, it would. And if I'm lucky, Mom just might get that second daughter she's been campaigning for," he added with a wink. He sauntered out, leaving his dad with his mouth hanging open.

Maya kept checking her phone all weekend hoping Ian would call. She loved him and missed him. But by Monday, she had given up all hope that the relationship could be salvaged. She had not heard anything from his company, either, and resigned herself to the fact that she would, most likely, end up having to rebuild her business again somewhere else. There was no way she could win the fight. And with economic times being the way they were, she would be lucky to survive the upheaval. Maya locked the shop and went home. She parked in her spot, started up the walkway and stopped short.

"What in the world?" She approached the mounds of white covering the grass in front of her door. Not believing her eyes, she bent and touched it just to be sure. "Snow."

"You said the only thing missing from Christmas was snow. I took a chance that it wouldn't melt before you got home in this sixty-degree weather."

She turned to face Ian. "I can't believe… How did you…"

Ian slowly walked toward her. "I had it brought down from the mountains. I'd bring you the mountain if I could."

"I love you," she blurted.

He stopped. "What did you say?"

Her heart raced with excitement and she felt like screaming it to the heavens. "I love you."

He closed the remaining distance, hauled her into his arms and crushed his mouth against hers. She didn't care that they were standing on the sidewalk, only that he was here.

"Can we go inside?"

"Yes, of course."

Ian followed her a few steps, then stopped. "I need to get something out of my car. I'll be right back."

She watched him jog back down the path and smiled. He came back holding two tubes. "What's in there?"

"Let's go in and I'll show you."

They entered and he unrolled the papers from the first tube and placed it on the coffee table. She realized immediately that it was an architectural blueprint. She took a seat on the sofa and leaned forward to study the drawing. There were several rooms with one word written in each one. She scooted closer. "What is this? Why do all the rooms have my name in them?"

He lowered himself to one knee next to her. "Because this is the blueprint to my heart, and you own every room inside it."

Her heart stopped for a second before starting up again.

He withdrew a small box from his pocket and opened it. The princess-cut center stone was surrounded by round accent diamonds with elaborate vintage sculpting along the sides and front. "Marry me, Maya. I love you and I will honor, protect and cherish you all the days of my life. And I'll do my best to turn your every dream into reality."

She was off the couch and in his arms as soon as the words were off his tongue. "Yes, yes, yes!" She lifted his face and kissed him with a passion that left them both gasping for air.

Still trying to catch his breath, Ian said, "I have one more thing to show you."

Maya eased back onto the sofa and waited while he opened the second tube. More blueprints. These were far more complicated than the first set.

"This is the condo project."

"Oh," she said dejectedly, the joy of the previous moment now waning.

Ian chuckled. "You don't have to sound so sad, sweetheart. I promise you'll like it." He pointed to a section. "I redesigned the project to add corporate space."

Her heart rate kicked up again. "What does that mean?"

"It means that Maya's Sweet Spot will not be relocated. I presented this to the investors earlier and they approved it. There will also be a minimarket and a dry cleaner's."

She brought her hands to her mouth and tried to process what he was saying.

"I also took the liberty of redesigning the shop, to expand it a little and give you room to add a few tables and maybe a coffee or tea bar, so people can sit and enjoy their treats. You may have to close a few days to get it done, but—"

She launched herself at him again and held him tight. "I don't know what to say. Thank you, thank you."

"I love you so much, baby. Whatever you want, I'll get it if it's in my power."

Tears streamed down her face. She caressed his face and held his gaze intently. "I just want you, Ian Jeffries. I love you." And he owned every room in her heart, too.

Epilogue

Two years later

Maya took a slow tour around her newly designed shop. "I can't believe it," she whispered over and over.

"Girl, your hubby did his *thing* with this shop!" Rhonda said, coming to stand next to her.

"Yes, he did." Ian had designed the space to include a dozen or so tables and the coffee and tea bar, and made sure she had Wi-Fi for those patrons who wanted to enjoy their pastries while working. Her kitchen had also been enlarged with an additional oven and more counter work space. Maya had never thought she could be this happy.

"Do you know how many orders we've gotten for Christmas?" Rhonda had been working overtime to create brochures and postcards for every resident in the six hundred-unit property.

"I can imagine. I'm glad I hired Phoebe full-time."

"With all these orders, you may have to hire some part-time help for the holidays." Rhonda nudged Maya. "Your sexy husband is coming in the door. Girl, the way he's looking at you, I hope he doesn't burn the place down before we have the grand opening. I'm going in the back to help Phoebe. Hi, Ian. Bye, Ian."

Maya chuckled and watched Rhonda disappear around the corner.

"Does this meet with your approval, Mrs. Jeffries?"

She spun around at the sound of Ian's voice and smiled. "It more than meets my approval, Mr. Jeffries. It's incredible," she said, spreading her arms and gesturing around the shop. "I don't know how to thank you."

Ian closed the distance between them and pulled her into his embrace. He placed a tender kiss on her lips. "I know the perfect way to thank me."

She looped her arms around his neck and gave him a sultry smile. "Is that right?"

He nodded and a wolfish gleam lit his eyes. Bending close to her ear, he whispered, "Bring home two cups of the black-and-white parfait and I'll show you."

She remembered every vivid detail of their first night together, and just like then, heat thrummed through her. "That sounds like an offer I can't refuse."

"I love you, Maya Jeffries. You were and still are the best Christmas gift I ever received. I can't wait to have you under my tree again."

"Neither can I." She pulled his head down and kissed him with all the love she felt flowing through her heart. Of all the gifts he had given her, his love was the sweetest one.

* * * * *

A redeeming passion

KIMANI ROMANCE

LINDSAY EVANS

BARE PLEASURES

MIAMI STRONG

LINDSAY EVANS

BARE
PLEASURES

After Alexander Diallo's youthful indiscretions follow him to Miami, he is blackmailed into romancing a stranger. Then the successful computer engineer starts falling for Noelle Palmer and wants to turn the charade into a permanent union. Can Lex convince her that love can erase all past mistakes?

MIAMI STRONG

• • • • • • ● ● ● • • • •

Available November 2016!

"Every page is dripping with emotion, making it all too easy for readers to lose themselves in the story and fall in love with the characters."
—*RT Book Reviews* on *Snowy Mountain Nights*

HARLEQUIN®
www.Harlequin.com

KPLE474

In the key of love

Kianna
Alexander

Joi Lewis's security firm is vying for a contract with an international bank. First she must prove her trustworthiness to the gorgeous Marco Alvarez. She dares him to open up in ways he never has. But after a safety breach, they must fight to keep their passionate duet alive.

THE
GENTLEMEN
OF QUEEN CITY

Available November 2016!

"A page-turner… Readers can lose themselves in the story."
—*RT Book Reviews* on *This Tender Melody*

www.Harlequin.com

KPKA475

A love worth waiting for

Sherelle Green

KIMANI™ ROMANCE

Waiting for **Summer** by

BARE SOPHISTICATION

Sherelle Green

Waiting for **Summer**

Summer Dupree has high hopes for the new Bare Sophistication boutique's grand opening in Miami. Then she spots a familiar face—fashion photographer Aiden Chase. Now her childhood friend is ready to create a future together. Can he turn his passion for Summer into a love story for the ages?

BARE SOPHISTICATION

Available November 2016!

"The love scenes are steamy and passionate, and the storyline is fast-paced and well-rounded." —*RT Book Reviews* on *If Only For Tonight*

 **HARLEQUIN®**
™ www.Harlequin.com

KPSG476

REQUEST YOUR FREE BOOKS!

2 FREE NOVELS
PLUS 2 FREE GIFTS!

KIMANI™
ROMANCE

Love's ultimate destination!

YES! Please send me 2 FREE Harlequin® Kimani™ Romance novels and my 2 FREE gifts (gifts are worth about $10). After receiving them, if I don't wish to receive any more books, I can return the shipping statement marked "cancel." If I don't cancel, I will receive 4 brand-new novels every month and be billed just $5.44 per book in the U.S. or $5.99 per book in Canada. That's a savings of at least 16% off the cover price. It's quite a bargain! Shipping and handling is just 50¢ per book in the U.S. and 75¢ per book in Canada.* I understand that accepting the 2 free books and gifts places me under no obligation to buy anything. I can always return a shipment and cancel at any time. Even if I never buy another book, the two free books and gifts are mine to keep forever.

168/368 XDN GH4P

Name _____ (PLEASE PRINT)

Address _____ Apt. #

City _____ State/Prov. _____ Zip/Postal Code

Signature (if under 18, a parent or guardian must sign)

Mail to the **Reader Service:**

IN U.S.A.: P.O. Box 1867, Buffalo, NY 14240-1867
IN CANADA: P.O. Box 609, Fort Erie, Ontario L2A 5X3

**Want to try two free books from another line?
Call 1-800-873-8635 or visit www.ReaderService.com.**

* Terms and prices subject to change without notice. Prices do not include applicable taxes. Sales tax applicable in N.Y. Canadian residents will be charged applicable taxes. Offer not valid in Quebec. This offer is limited to one order per household. Not valid for current subscribers to Harlequin® Kimani™ Romance books. All orders subject to credit approval. Credit or debit balances in a customer's account(s) may be offset by any other outstanding balance owed by or to the customer. Please allow 4 to 6 weeks for delivery. Offer available while quantities last.

Your Privacy—The Reader Service is committed to protecting your privacy. Our Privacy Policy is available online at www.ReaderService.com or upon request from the Reader Service.

We make a portion of our mailing list available to reputable third parties that offer products we believe may interest you. If you prefer that we not exchange your name with third parties, or if you wish to clarify or modify your communication preferences, please visit us at www.ReaderService.com/consumerschoice or write to us at Reader Service Preference Service, P.O. Box 9062, Buffalo, NY 14240-9062. Include your complete name and address.

KROM15

Turn your love of reading into rewards you'll love with

Harlequin My Rewards

**Join for FREE today at
www.HarlequinMyRewards.com**

Earn **FREE BOOKS** of your choice.

Experience **EXCLUSIVE OFFERS** and contests.

Enjoy **BOOK RECOMMENDATIONS**
selected just for you.

PLUS! Sign up now
and get **500** points
right away!

Earn **FREE** REWARDS
HarlequinMyRewards.com
Join Today!

MYR16R

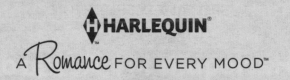

HARLEQUIN®

A *Romance* FOR EVERY MOOD™

JUST CAN'T GET ENOUGH?

Join our social communities
and talk to us online.

You will have access to the latest
news on upcoming titles and special
promotions, but most importantly,
you can talk to other fans about your
favorite Harlequin reads.

Harlequin.com/Community

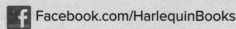

Facebook.com/HarlequinBooks

Twitter.com/HarlequinBooks

Pinterest.com/HarlequinBooks

HSOCIAL

SPECIAL EXCERPT FROM

*Everything schoolteacher Morgan Hill loves is in her
hometown of Temptation, Virginia—her twins,
her students and the charming community center
where she's staging their holiday play. But now the
building's new owner, Grayson Taylor, is putting sexy
visions into Morgan's head, making the young widow
long for a future even Santa couldn't deliver...*

Read on for a sneak peek at
ONE MISTLETOE WISH,
the first exciting installment in author A.C. Arthur's
***TAYLORS OF TEMPTATION** series!*

Her back was to the window and Gray moved to stand
in front of her. He rubbed the backs of his fingers lightly
over her cheek.

"Those buildings mean something to you, don't they?"
he asked her.

She shrugged, shifting from one foot to the other as if
his proximity was making her nervous. Being this close
to her was making him hot and aroused. He wondered if
that was what she was really feeling, as well.

"This town means something to me. There are good
people here and we're trying to do good things."

KPEXP1116

"That's what my mother used to say," Gray continued, loving the feel of her smooth skin beneath his touch. "Temptation was a good place. Love, family, loyalty. They meant something to the town. Always. That's what she used to tell us when we were young. But that was after the show, after my father found something better outside of this precious town of Temptation."

Gray could hear the sting to his tone, felt the tensing of his muscles that came each time he thought about Theodor Taylor and all that he'd done to his family. Yes, Gray had buried his father two months ago. He'd followed the old man's wishes right down to the ornate gold handles on the slate-gray casket, but Gray still hated him. He still despised any man that could walk away from his family without ever looking back.

"Show me something better," he found himself saying as he stared down into Morgan's light brown eyes. "Show me what this town is really about and maybe I'll reconsider selling."

"Are you making a bargain with me?" she asked. "Because if you are, I don't know what to say. I'm not used to wheeling and dealing big businessmen like you."

"I'm asking you to give me a reason why I shouldn't sell those buildings. Just one will do. If you can convince me—"

She was already shaking her head. "I won't sleep with you. If that is what you mean by *convince* you."

Don't miss ONE MISTLETOE WISH
by A.C. Arthur, available December 2016
wherever Harlequin® Kimani Romance™
books and ebooks are sold.

WITHDRAWN
FROM
LONDON
PUBLIC LIBRARY

Copyright © 2016 by Artist Arthur

KPEXP1116